THEY DRINK OUR BLOOD

LUCY LEITNER

Copyright © 2025 by Lucy Leitner

First Edition

All rights reserved

ISBN: 978-1-940250-70-0

Cover Art by Nero Art Ink
  http://www.neroartink.com/

Interior Layout by Lori Michelle
  www.TheAuthorsAlley.com

Printed in the United States of America

Visit us on the web at:
www.bloodboundbooks.net
https://www.bloodgutsandstory.com/

A WOMAN WALKS into a bar.

It's not a swanky bar, not the type of place where the bartender slides her a cocktail with a single giant ice cube, meeting her look of confusion with "It's from the man at the end of the bar." No man raises his glass with a smile and a wink, hoping she'll thank him. No man does that for Lisa. Not anymore. She's too old for the blonde to be real and not old enough for it to appear fake. Not yet.

They still talk to her, though later in the evening than they did in years past. They usually start with the tattoos, the obvious ones, the ones you can see at the bar even during Pittsburgh's frigid winters when the perpetual gray keeps most at home to combat the seasonal lows with the highs of conversation among loved ones.

The black brushes crossing the back of her right hand—her beer hand—at the wrist start the conversation.

"So, let me guess; you're an artist."

"Right on," Lisa would say, and she'd force herself into silence to await the next question. Be an enigma, a bit mysterious so they'll want to learn more. That's what her mom suggested when dealing with men and what Camille said about dealing with patrons at the gallery. Tease. In this situation—which had repeated itself so many times over her past two decades as an artist—both applied.

"So, what do you paint? I'm guessing you're a painter since you don't have a potter's wheel tattoo or nothing."

She would like to say a potter is an artisan, but both of her older female influences would say she's being pedantic, so Lisa says what she always says because it's her only answer.

"I paint shapes."

"Shapes? Like squares?"

"Mostly. Some circles. An occasional rhombus."

"Ever paint a hexagon?"

"Once, but I didn't like it, so ever since, I've limited my art to four edges."

"So, shapes . . . Why? Doesn't art have to mean something? What are you saying with a square?"

"That's up to you." And she would repeat Camille's words that instilled such profundity into what is essentially a bird's-eye view

1

of a home in Flatland. "My art isn't about me or my vision of the world. It's not about me trying to tell you anything. I'm not trying to say the world is a square or that's how I see myself. It's about you. When you look at an orange square receding into a black vignette, what do you see? How do you feel? How is the experience different from gazing into the blue square that seems to burst from the textured yellow? Art should always be about the viewer's interpretation. Art is nothing if it doesn't mean something to the beholder. I'm just the messenger. It's what you get out of it that matters."

Sometimes they would ask to see her work. Some, she'd direct to her website, which shows no contact information but a form that sends emails into the abyss, if she didn't recall the inquiring name when the Straub wore off. That won't be an option when the hosting expires next month if she doesn't find a reliable source of income and the inspiration to be an artist—who gives impassioned speeches about the self-reflecting nature of the painted quadrilateral—again.

Some she would direct to Amadeo, Camille's gallery, but when her decade-long employer and most consistent show host couldn't sell enough squares or any other works to make up for those pre-vaccine doldrums, her referrals dried up along with her cash flow. Others, the rare few, she would offer to show her art that evening— her art and herself, after the male patron's flattering interpretation of the latest canvas drying on the easel. It rarely came to more than an awkward goodbye in the morning and a promise to think about the square for his living room.

When a woman walks into a bar alone, the automatic assumption is she's meeting someone. A husband, boyfriend, maybe even a tryst. Or just a girlfriend, for a relatively quiet place to catch up. Because this bar, with the exception of the national news broadcast on the single TV mounted high on the wall, is pretty quiet as bars on Carson Street go. But when the door opens and Lisa doesn't look up with a hopeful glance, the college kids slumming it at the pool table in the back room can notice she's just here by herself. If they notice her at all.

"Straub's kicked," Jodi says. The bartender could be any of the women depicted in realist paintings, waist and wrists made thick from swinging a scythe in the fields. Maybe Millet's subjects were her ancestors, until the cities sprang up around them and their haggard faces became the other half that Lisa studied in that old photography book. Jodi's toil may have moved indoors, but it keeps her just as busy as her predecessors. Like them, she has no time to consider a more profound purpose than the everyday grind that contributes, in some small but essential way, to the homeostasis humanity needs to keep progressing.

"That's OK. Just a coffee anyway."

Jodi always has a pot brewing to keep her going through the 2 a.m. closing time.

When a woman sits at the bar alone and it becomes clear she'll stay alone, the assumption is she's an alcoholic. Sipping her brand X black coffee, Lisa cuts a sadder figure. She's not here for the drink. She's here for the company. And the stools next to her are empty. That is, if the nine other patrons—those dulling their senses with bottom-shelf liquor at the bar and the four college-age youths whooping in dramatic celebration of a sunken eight ball—notice.

And who would notice Lisa at this point? For the past 25 years, she's been lurking in these bars, in the community meetings, finding your voter card at the polling station. She's never been on stage at any of the old concert venues that closed, never been commissioned to paint any of her art on the walls of this bar, Jake's Mistake, or any others.

Kids like the ones in the back never notice. While they're concerned with the next Jager shot and how good the brunette's ass looks in those jeans, maybe the slightest worry about the exam next week, they don't notice the world falling apart, let alone someone like Lisa. They stumble through the streets, sometimes barefoot, no concern the bad element will make them victims tonight. The victims on the news may as well be characters on a sitcom. Things like that couldn't happen to them. They're real; the people those things happened to are not. They can't be. Because things like that don't really happen. Not to them. At least, not that they know.

Those college kids aren't the problem. They're not the ones mugging the locals after last call, not the ones who killed those people in Ohio, Colorado, and Alabama. Still, those kids aren't doing anything to stop it. They're not paying attention.

The other lonely people in the bar are missing what's right in front of them, too. Their attention wrapped in whatever they're trying to forget, they fail to notice their beers are flat, their glasses musty. Even Lisa's looming obligation is pulling her away from the real story.

How could she be expected to work in the midst of this mayhem?

"Oh, now I see why this place is dead. There's a Pens game on, and you're playing depressing news." Mike emerges from the men's room to shove his way behind the bar with the authority only an owner who wants everyone to know what he owns has. He tosses his Miller High Life bottle in the trash can as if he's at the free-throw line.

Lisa opens her mouth to say Jake's Mistake is dead because Mike hasn't bothered to cover the yellowed, cracked paint with a new pigment or with new decor aside from the Budweiser mirror some long-lost frat brother known now only as Barracuda stole back in the early 2000s. She shuts her mouth, knowing Mike will retort that Jake's wouldn't survive a makeover if it meant customers assumed their shots and beers wouldn't be at shot-and-beer prices anymore. Most don't spend their lives immersed in the visual, discerning a hidden meaning in forms.

Besides, as Mike has said, everyone knows the important decor is seated on the barstools.

But like the stools on which they slouch, the forms of the living female decor are now wrinkled, cracked, and stained. To Lisa, shapes have morphed like a Salvador Dalí painting: melting timekeepers, in this case hourglasses swelling at the center so all the sand dumps to the bottom at once. Such is the plummet of the barfly. No slow descent to time, just a glance into the Budweiser mirror in one of the few areas without a grimy frost. The first look is like a Monet at a distance that upon further examination reveals little bulbous areas in the flesh that don't correspond with the underlying structure.

Little black dots on the nose, dark Cézanne brushstrokes separating now-distinct areas of flesh. Mike is right: Lisa and Walter, in his suit and bowler hat on the other side of the bar regaling anyone within earshot of his days as a secret agent for the U.S. government, are fixtures. They make up an organic art installation. And what is the meaning? That eventually who and where become the same? That they're little more than furnishings for the next generation passing through? Scene setting for those kids in the back playing pool on the one withered table?

After all, it's more interesting decor than what Mike would pay for. More for those kids to tell their friends, give them FOMO the next time they're invited out to a night of slumming. They've just gotta meet the old barfly. It's interactive. Experiential. As Instagrammable as wings painted on the side of a derelict building. Lisa is a creator becoming the created, the artist becoming grotesque art, a gargoyle on the drainage gutter of a once grand cathedral. When did that happen?

"Like the Pens aren't just as depressing as the news these days, Mike," Jodi says. "And I wanna see more about this story. There's a woman with her throat slashed in an alley in Nashville."

"You know, it's bad enough those kids are out of control and scaring everyone from coming down to my bar. We don't need the damn news convincing the few people who are willing to leave their houses and risk getting knocked down and embarrassed on social media to go right back home."

"But this was in Nashville—"

"Don't matter. Goddamn kids are a menace everywhere. Why can't they shotgun beers at a bonfire like we did back in the day? We weren't hurting anyone. The cops don't come down on them soon, you won't have a job." Mike turns to Lisa. "And you won't have a spot that lets you sit here all night without ordering anything."

His eyes meet hers, and she does her best to hide them behind the lids. He's looking right at her, but what is he seeing? As his face grows redder, it appears to take a different shape, mouth relaxing, nose swelling, eyes shrinking into tiny, sparkling marbles. But the sparkle is as lifeless as stripper glitter. It's not the soul; it's a deliberate way to mask the absence of one.

Lisa has seen this look before. It was on the face of her college friend Berty right before he'd get them tossed from one bar and hitchhike to the next. It is no longer Berty's face, but that of whatever demon lived inside Berty that the alcohol summoned to the surface. Or maybe it is the true Berty, and this is the true face. The Berty Lisa knew and loved was just a mask to disguise what society deemed illegal and immoral. Either way, for Lisa it meant an adventure. A risk. Sometimes Berty would slip a $10 bill to a DJ to play his song next in karaoke, and Lisa's mood was as light as a Calder mobile. Other times, when a car was involved, she felt the doom of being inside a Zdzisław Beksiński scene. But Lisa followed him, never knowing if the next scene would be one from Goya's court paintings or one from his black period.

THEY DRINK OUR BLOOD

That's the face Mike wears now as he perches on the ledge of his bar. That face is the reason it's called demon alcohol.

Lisa pulls a $5 bill from her wallet and sticks it under her near-empty mug. "That's a good point. I gotta get logged in." Lisa steps off her stool. She could spend another dollar, buy a bag of Fritos, but Mike would still be there.

"Aw shit, I didn't mean leave."

"Let her be, Mike. She's gotta pick up some fares. Can't have people walking around when the kids are out."

The woman leaves the bar alone.

And she thinks, maybe it would be safer to leave with a stranger. At least he would be an adult. The damage these kids could inflict is far scarier than anything they'd detect from a swab at the free clinic.

You're never totally safe in the city. Lisa knows that, but in 20 years in this part of town, she's never felt her heart beat through her chest strolling down the sidewalk. That's for neophytes, kids right off the farm overcoming years of assumptions that muggers lurk on every corner, that a wrong turn takes you, as Lisa sees it, to artist Walter Sickert's *Camden Town*. When you've been here as long as Lisa, you know the old man in the tattered field general's jacket isn't shouting at you. And some nights, when the kids form their threatening masses like packs of bloodthirsty wolves, you're glad he's there to distract them.

The pundits say the stress of anticipating a horrible event is worse than the experience itself. Her heart pounds, her breath shortens. But where are the teenagers? No Cheshire cat smiles to taunt patrons of nonexistent sidewalk cafés. No porcine savages shouting with cracking voices through megaphones the modern slurs that older generations don't understand until the evening news translates. No masked hormonal lunatics linking arms in a crosswalk and challenging drivers to a high-stakes game of chicken, mutually assured destruction. That's been every night in the South Side and in America for the past three weeks, according to news reports.

So why not tonight? Is this generation finally lost to its great war, a TikTok challenge gone awry? The last Lisa heard, Tide Pods and cyborgs were just urban legends designed to scare parents, but this *grande peur* has been different. She's known people who have seen it. She can corroborate it.

So again, her heart pounds and her breath shortens even though the only people close by are a trio of college girls no more threatening than their mom jeans and white crop tops would convey. No irony in the festival look up top and the PTA meeting below, just fashion. It's not like the mockery of the teenagers pairing their parents' super-wide-leg jeans and spaghetti-strap tank tops with propeller hats.

Are these John Singer Sargent's little girls with the paper lanterns all grown up to hold each other's beach waves back after too many hard seltzers? *Les Demoiselles d'Avignon* of Pablo Picasso's imagination subverted with innocence. When they're Lisa's age, they'll squeeze in time for each other at parties selling BPA-free Tupperware or woven baskets with medicinal properties, not drinking black coffee like a nighthawk in a sloppy dive bar alone.

In their rococo frivolity, they don't hear the rumblings.

Lisa does.

These girls may think they'll always have someone to link in their arm, to be vigilant for them. They'll never need to be *Liberty Leading the People,* but Lisa might, even if it's just Lady Liberty forcing her way to her car with no one following her. So the three girls don't hear it coming. The tsunami cracking down and washing over the streets and sidewalks with such force it threatens to carry the tables and chairs away into the violent surf. Kids wailing like extinct warriors, some laughing.

It's like a school choir: voices in all pitches and timbres meshing into a wall of incomprehensible sound. And piercing through the amplifying din like an errant screech in an orchestra violin solo, some screams, the kind that the clichés say turn your blood into cottage cheese.

A cacophony of chaos. The kids in the throng run, oblivious to any obstacles in their path or just indifferent. Phones raised, live streaming the mayhem as they barrel past the few pedestrians too slowed by drink to dodge the tide. Lisa ducks around the corner, plastering herself against the wall of Jake's Mistake, watching the wave of destructive adolescence.

She doesn't know how many of them there are. It's like guessing the jellybeans in a jar, if the jellybeans are all caterwauling and charging at you. And even if she tries to count, she watches enough news to know eyewitness accounts are unreliable at best.

So Lisa waits against the wall, pretending to be the spray-paint art that comes right after the microbrewery stage of urban renewal, watching until the last of the kids run by. The whole spectacle must take no more than a minute.

The crescendo of thundering wails fades for the next blocks to experience while a shrill shriek fills its void. Lisa rounds the corner back to Carson. One of the pre-Raphaelite trio is plopped on the ground, grasping the side of her neck. Blood dyes her already multihued hair. A deep scarlet forms tendrils over her chest, staining her white top and her white chest. It's as incongruous as a lobster telephone. She's the one screaming. One of her friends pulls off her nearly identical top and presses it against the neck wound.

From her art school anatomy lessons, Lisa knows it's a surface laceration, didn't nick an artery. But these girls are as terrified as Edvard Munch on a stroll, panicked and now semiclothed.

"Hey! Are you OK?" Lisa asks. "Why don't you come into Jake's Mistake to clean her off? They've got bar rags and such and I think a first aid kit, too. Yeah, yeah, they do, 'cause a while back one of the bartenders—Amelia, she quit a few weeks ago, probably because she wasn't making much on tips with so few customers— anyway, she cut herself real bad when she dropped the shot too hard into a car bomb, and some crazy reaction happened and the pint glass shattered. And yeah, I remember Jodi grabbing that first aid kit after using a bar rag to stop the bleeding like you're doing here, so I know you can get her all cleaned up at Jake's."

During Lisa's *megillah*, the bleeding girl stops wailing, realizing she isn't going to die tonight, and now presses the shirt against her neck while her friends help her from the sidewalk.

"It's OK. We're nursing students. We're taking her home," the shirtless blonde says.

"Thanks, though," says the lucky one who has retained her shirt and all five liters of blood in her veins.

Clinging to one another for comfort or to hide the now skimpy attire, the girls turn off Carson, making their way to wherever they reside until they graduate. To them, this neighborhood will never be anything more than a liminal space. It will never be their home where they can walk into a bar alone, a bar that provides a safe space with its policy of carding all who enter.

"Another coffee?" Jodi asks as Lisa reclaims her seat.

"No. Pint of Yuengling."

THEY DRINK OUR BLOOD

The morning riders are better anyway. Better tips, less chance of having to clock out to clean up vomit. When the sun comes up, the South Side violence abates. No lingering carnage, just the litter of drunks like tumbleweeds in the lonely streets while the revelers try to sleep off their hangovers. Better conversation in the ride share.

"You partying down here last night?" Lisa asks.

"It's that obvious?" The oversize Pitt hoodie nearly covers the girl's miniskirt. Her heels sit with her on the black cloth back seat of the Chevy HHR. The ride of shame.

"Just glad you're OK is all. With all the violence down here. You didn't get caught in the stampede, did you?"

"Huh? Stampede? No, we just hit the Grail."

"The Grail?" Lisa eyes the passenger through the rearview. The girl can't be much more than 100 pounds, and she has the face of a naïf. To survive a place like the Grail, at least from what Lisa has heard, you need the confidence of a woman who picnics in the nude among clothed men. "Oh, I'm so glad to see you made it out in one piece."

"Why?"

"You don't know? For the past two years that place has been a nuisance. A stabbing. A couple reports of assault in the bathrooms. Please don't tell me you drank from the chalice."

"The big grail behind the bar? No, just seltzer."

"Good girl. But remember, you got lucky this time. You shouldn't be going to nuisance clubs like that when it's so dangerous these days."

"So where do you recommend?" she asks. "My friends and I come down here most every Saturday night."

"Well, there's O'Malley's. Been here since 1989 and not one stabbing. Jake's Mistake. Used to be Ledbetter's. I can't say it's the same since old man Ledbetter died, but the new owner, Mike, hasn't changed the decor or nothing. Kominski's, but you gotta be OK with smoke."

"Aren't those all old-man bars?" The girl in the back seat scrunches her nose, as if the mere mention of those tragically un-hip establishments makes her need a chaser.

"You gotta stay outta the places the kids wanna go. It's the kids wreaking all the havoc. I tell you what; they may look grimy, but that's because they've got nothing to hide. Those glitzy joints like the Grail use a shiny veneer so you won't see the warning signs. Like hanging a Botticelli in a haunted house."

"Huh?"

"It's to trick you into thinking it's safe because it's pretty. But it's a lie."

"My friends aren't gonna wanna hit up a bunch of dive bars."

"OK. The MaleBox."

"That's a gay bar."

"And you're guaranteed a good night without anyone slipping something in your drink."

"Thanks. I'll keep that in mind."

Lisa opens her mouth to speak but sees in the mirror the girl has shifted her eyes down on her phone, ending the conversation. In any other situation, Lisa may keep pressing the issue or even start a new line of communication, but unwanted dialog can mean a star deduction. She never approaches ride-share driving with the passion she had thrown at her squares in the early years of her career, but lower rankings in this industry means less money that Lisa can't afford to lose.

"You've gotta support the good spots left in this neighborhood. You see a group of kids out later than any sensible curfew, you head in the other direction."

"I'm a teacher," says the new fare in the back seat. She's older than the barefoot girl Lisa dropped off in the cheaper part of the mountain that looms over the South Side. And this one is dressed in her own clothes, presumably having summoned Lisa to her own home. "You don't have to tell me twice."

"No kidding. What grade?"

"Middle school. Math."

"So is this whole generation screwed?"

"No, I don't think so—"

"You gotta see a lot of guns at school."

"Haven't seen one yet."

"Metal detectors must have caught 'em. Good thing you got those in there, though I would've probably freaked out as a kid seeing them in my school."

"I teach up in the suburbs. We don't have metal detectors."

"Clear bags?"

"No."

THEY DRINK OUR BLOOD

"Aren't you scared walking in every day?"

"Honestly, no. The worst I've seen are fist fights. Like when I was back in school 100 years ago. A bully shoves a smart kid into a locker. Girls pull hair."

"That's normal?"

"Oh, come on. You never had a fight when you were young?" The woman in the back seat raises her eyebrows over the thick blue frames of her glasses.

"When I was that age, I definitely wasn't coming down to the South Side. I grew up not 10 miles from here, and I didn't even know this place existed. We were in the woods with a keg and some joints and Sublime cracking on the boombox until the battery died. The only thing we ever needed a knife for was to cut into the beer to shotgun it."

"What's Sublime?" the new, uninterested, young voice says from the back seat.

"I guess they're not on TikTok."

"Everything's been on TikTok at one point." A peek into the rearview shows the morning's third rider hidden behind blue hair, scrolling on a phone. It's rewired their brains, Lisa thinks, just as the news says. Like they're bifurcated; a foot in the real world and a foot in the digital one.

The app on Lisa's phone mounted to the dashboard shows she's arrived at the destination, a burger joint in the suburbs, not unlike the neighborhood where she spent her youth.

"Thanks," the passenger says, opening the door. "You should give TikTok a try. It's not as scary as you think."

Of course it's not. A stampede is entertainment when viewed on a tiny screen, terrifying when you're corporeally immersed in it.

Lisa ends the ride and swipes out of the app.

Facebook's little red dot says 27. Lisa's notifications show all 27 are updates from the South Side Down Low group. A news story sits atop her feed.

DENNING DENIED. ACTOR FIT TO BE "TYED" WHEN REFUSED ENTRY TO LOCAL BAR.

Actor Ty Denning found out last night that a blue check mark does not constitute a valid form of ID.

Bar employees said that around 10:30 p.m., Denning, 24, attempted to enter the MaleBox on Pittsburgh's South Side without identification. According to bouncer Thor Cole, when he asked to see identification, Denning instead "proudly displayed his Instagram account."

"He kept talking about a blue check mark," said Cole, 51. "I said it was checkmate if he didn't have his ID."

It was then that bar patron Todd Ellis said Denning "threw a full-on hissy fit." So Ellis, 34, started filming from inside the bar. In Ellis's footage, the actor, in town filming "Working Stiffs," demanded, "Don't you know who I am?" to which Cole responded, "No."

A spokesman for the actor denied the incident took place, claiming it was an impostor pretending to be Denning.

"That's why he didn't have ID," the spokesman said.

Pittsburghers aren't buying it. In the two weeks Denning has been in town, this is the second incident that has diminished any goodwill toward the Netflix star. In an interview last week with TMZ regarding filming a scene on one of the city's 446 bridges, he quipped he "would jump off one if [he] had to live in this town."

Cole said this remark did not factor into his refusal of entry at the MaleBox, claiming he hadn't heard of the incident. Nor was he aware the actor had been banned from two of Hollywood's men's bars, the bouncer said.

At approximately 10:45 p.m., bar back Justin Mazzullo says, Denning attempted to force his way through the rear entry when Mazzullo was tossing a bag of trash into a dumpster.

"We may be a gay bar, but, like our patrons, we require consent for entry," said MaleBox owner Jack "Lips" Gamshe, 72.

Lisa smirks. Lips. What would South Side be without people like him? She clicks out of the browser and back to Facebook.

128 comments in the group thread under the article.

Fuck that Hollywood asshole.

Entitled prick.

He better watch his back on bridges, just saying.

So sad. He was a cute kid.

Pedo.

Oh yeah, I'm really going out on a limb here saying a child star was cute. They better put me on a watchlist.

She continues scrolling through the feed, in the virtual world, her eyes may as well have turned to clouds, until a honk jolts her back into the real world of the loading zone. Lisa jams the HHR into drive, contemplating how fame puts an undue importance on events. A routine bouncing supersedes a near riot. Sure, the anonymous mob of teenagers wasn't a massacre (this time), but it left more carnage than some star acting like he's in the 14th of his 15 minutes. The media are so infatuated with celebrity that they miss the real story, is Lisa's conclusion as she parks the HHR outside the old warehouse turned subsidized artist studios. She turns her key in the front door, makes her way to the ancient elevator, pulls the cage shut, and rides to her studio on the fourth floor.

Lisa almost jumps from the couch. Maybe it's the news anchor's graphic description of the 38-year-old bride-to-be's head lolling from exposed tendons, the spinal column severed, the blood pooling in the alley in Nashville that has her on edge. Or the shock of the rare buzz at her door and Koko's bark.

"The suspect, described by the witness as a male with blond hair who appeared to be in his teens, was seen fleeing the scene toward Broadway."

Another buzz, cutting through the broadcast with as much violence as whatever beast tore into poor Emily Beckworth neck. Yes, Lisa heard that right: the unfamiliar signal of a visitor asking to be let in. She mutes the volume, hits the closed-caption button; everybody knows the chyrons tell just the headlines, and who wants to be the person who knows only the big picture? Lisa is beyond that. After hours of broadcasts by three major networks—everyone knows you don't get the real story from one, just like a reporter doesn't get all the information from a single source—Lisa and Emily have moved past that. Though they never met, Lisa has watched so much material and done so much research on her phone that they are past the "what's your favorite color?" stage of their relationship.

She stands, the sudden movement sending the blood from her head to her finally moving legs. Shaking her head to get the proverbial stars out of her eyes, she tosses the remote on the couch. She dutifully restrains her pit bull mix, her sworn protector from visitors and deliveries, and opens the door a crack. The building predates the need for peepholes.

Koko lurches her 70-pound body through the crack, standing on her furry hind legs as the bare human legs in the hallway squat down. The dog and neighbor are eye level, as friends should be.

"Well, hello, Koko, you little sweetheart. Who's my favorite girl? Yes, you're my favorite girl." Sonia rubs Koko behind the ears as the dog gives her version of a hug, her paws resting on flannel-covered shoulders.

"C'mon Koko. You can cuddle more if you let her in." Lisa pulls the dog away from the door.

Sonia stands, brushing the tan fur from her open flannel and, with more struggle, the ribbed white tank top beneath it. The fur mingles with the fringe of her denim cut-offs.

THEY DRINK OUR BLOOD

"Excuse Koko. She's a little pent-up today. I've been so busy I didn't realize we haven't been out since I got back from driving. I think that was around 11, and now it's what?" Lisa looks at her old Fitbit, ignoring the meager 1,200 steps logged today. "Eight-thirty. Oh damn. No wonder she rushed to the door. I gotta take her out. I was just all wrapped up in—"

"Were you painting?" Sonia looks around the open studio—600 square feet—that makes little distinction between living and working other than the head-shop tapestries cordoning off the sleeping area. The couch, coffee table, and TV sit almost in the center. Fanning out are all manner of scavenged tables covered with easels and stacks of decades of orange-square paintings. The spaces merge with the kitchenette and the sole sink for cleaning both dishes and brushes, though tonight its only occupants are cereal bowls and coffee mugs.

The only item of real value—because her own career has been on the posthumous-recognition track—is the one that serves no purpose, art that tried to be anything but, Man Ray's 1921 Dada object *The Gift*. The antique iron—back from a time when irons were iron—with the nails stuck to its base, undermining its utility, sits upright on a waist-high white cylinder that, like its charge, is a remnant from the Amadeo Gallery, Lisa's severance pay for 15 years of faithful service. Of the 5,000 made a half century after the original extemporaneous creation was lost, Lisa owns number 1,768. And even produced at that volume, its value exceeds the rest of the studio combined, plus a couple of months of subsidized rent.

"No, I've been learning about what happened in Nashville. You know Emily Beckworth was younger than me, by seven years? It's so sad. She'd been about to get married, which I know doesn't matter all that much to people like you and me because we've got our art and all and careers, but Emily had all that too, but she still wanted the whole domestic life, I guess, and it was just cut so short—"

"Who's Emily Beckworth?"

"You haven't heard?" Lisa points to the TV. "It's all over the news, Sonia. You gotta pay attention since we live down here. There's a lot of parallels to Nashville—"

"I've been working all day; I can't focus with all that yammering. I can only paint to music. You can paint to the news? I guess that makes sense . . . " Sonia trails off, but an interloper wouldn't notice because Lisa starts back in. Her words evoke a Boschian hellscape of kids running from the scene; fountains of blood; a near decapitation; city names of Akron, Louisville, Chicago. But the monotonous delivery, the matter-of-fact nature and the endless rambling make a story that references such an ear-catching word as "vampires" as bland as Lisa had heard gallery visitors describe her squares on the canvases. What were they saying? Were they trying to say anything? Did they have a purpose other than to adorn an eggshell wall and make their creator say she's an artist? Is their utter lack of substance a commentary on our collective obsession with the superfluous?

"The kid was running from the alley, and it was like I could see it, like when the orange square first popped into my head."

"So, you haven't been painting?"

"No. Honestly this whole thing with the kids—I tell you I saw it firsthand? Last night I stepped out of Jake's, and the mob was running down the sidewalk, everyone diving out of the way. These three young nurses—one of them got the flesh ripped from her neck. Torn right off. Some vicious kid during the fracas. She survived, and her head wasn't hanging off like poor Emily's, but still it's so similar, it's eerie. So the reason I've been all glued to the TV news today is the mob of kids and the neck wound connection and I think we maybe oughtta be concerned here. So, no, I haven't been painting because I'm thinking no one else has connected the dots yet and someone's gotta be vigilant and make sure no one in South Side becomes Emily Beckworth."

"So, since you're not painting, you'd be able to lend me some linseed oil? I want to get the first layer down tonight so it sets, and obviously all the stores are closed."

"Oh yeah, sure." Lisa walks to the metal shelf on the right-side wall, reaches through the cobwebs to the little slimy bottles. "I've got some of the series three oils right now. I like to mix in a little stand oil as well to get the high-glaze finish. Sometimes with this type I don't even need it, and this one by itself is a little thinner, but it can suit the purpose."

As Sonia takes the half-full bottle of amber liquid from Lisa's outstretched hand, she says, "I've got plenty of stand oil. What I get for going to the store on memory without a list. Thank you." She turns toward the door. Koko lets out a yelp and pushes against Sonia's legs for a final pet before farewell.

"Yeah, I always have a little inventory spreadsheet on my phone. You ever use Google Sheets?"

"Yes, I—" Sonia steps toward the exit, followed by the dog.

"I found a template online, and I—"

Koko barks at the door.

"Lisa, she really wants to go out."

"Oh yeah, OK. I better take her out. I guess I'm dreading it because it's a Saturday night and that's when the teens have been getting all wild, and I'm all shook up from the news stories and poor Emily Beckworth and—"

"Well, all the more reason to get out while it's still early-ish. Thanks for the oil. I'll get you back."

Before Lisa can get a word out, Sonia is nothing more than soft footsteps barely audible on the other side of the heavy door left over from the building's industrial days.

Lisa glances back at the TV, still silent, though the chyron is screaming, "Are your children being seduced by vampires?"

She takes a step toward the couch, but Koko's whimper calls her back to the door.

"OK, Koko, we're leaving. You better be quick since it's not safe for us out there anymore."

But Koko doesn't understand the news, doesn't even understand that the dogs in the commercials aren't actually in a small box inside her home, so to her, it's just outside, and everyone in Nashville still has their head. To Koko, it's not even Saturday night, maybe it's not even night. Unless night smells different from day. Maybe the unwrapped tampon that's been rolling around on the sidewalk since Tuesday has a special sun scent.

If it were up to Lisa, they'd walk back and forth in just the right intervals to keep the motion light on at the converted old warehouse's front doors where, if the kids ever reached it, she could shove the key into the lock and be safe behind glass.

But it's not up to Lisa.

Maybe if the W-A-L-K had happened two hours earlier when Koko first whimpered at the door, the dog would have been content to saunter through the cratered alley, past the dumpsters around the self-storage facility and back to the subsidized artists' lofts in 10 minutes, the boring part of the neighborhood with too little foot traffic for the kids to bother terrorizing. It would have been the last rays of autumn daylight then, maybe the indigo dusk.

Instead, Koko leads Lisa through the darkness. Sure, there are streetlights and porch lights and living room lights, but any dark is too dark for Lisa. Too dark for any adult who watches the news.

It was dark when Emily Beckworth's throat was slashed open and the bride-to-be was left gurgling and choking on her own blood, grasping her flayed trachea, desperate to seal those torn flaps of flesh until the oxygen stopped flowing to her brain and she asphyxiated alone on the asphalt.

It was dark when Dolores Mayburn's carotid artery was punctured and she ran, her screams little more than painful strains, through Lincoln Park, blood spraying from the wound like the greenery's sprinkler system.

It was dark when that young woman was trampled on Carson last night.

No, nothing good happens when the sun goes down. Not since the kids got infected with this monstrous mind virus.

Lisa tugs on the leash.

"C'mon, Koko, it's time to go home. It's late, and we shouldn't be out here now. I know we're usually out walking around, but that was before Nashville and Akron and Louisville and Chicago, and you know they're saying on the news it's gotta all be connected. You can't have four people nearly getting their heads torn off in the span of a week and it be random. So we gotta watch out."

But Koko understands a monologue about as well as she does a cable news broadcast, and so she forges forward, down 21st Street toward the neon glow of Carson. Though Lisa has double the weight (at least at her last physical, however many years ago), Koko's 70 pounds of stubborn dog, low center of gravity, and muscle are winning the tug-of-war.

Lisa's regaling Koko with more horror stories, reasons they don't need to go down to Carson, as if evening news "Do you know where your children are?" tactics will make up for her failure to finish the highly recommended canine training. The neon bar signs, the streetlights, the taillights in near gridlock as drunken pedestrians forget the red hand's universal meaning, and the traffic light in just about every intersection of the historic, narrow street still leave shadows.

A chessboard of vibrant businesses and vacant storefronts

alternates on each side of the street. And if you were caught in a black square, you may be a sacrificial pawn. It's just too risky these days, she tells Koko. The dog wasn't around seven years ago when there were more consecutive white squares. Lisa stares down at the sidewalk, so she doesn't slip in a puddle of vomit or trip on a discarded high heel. It used to be these party land mines were the biggest risk on a Saturday night.

Tonight she should be looking up, using her peripheral vision. Who cares about catching a toe on an uneven sidewalk slab and plummeting face-first into the smashed White Claw cans? Who cares if the can's pointed edges pierce her cheeks and as she wipes the blood she smears feathers from a dead pigeon into her wounds? They have shots for that. Seven dollars and a couple taps on an app can get her to three different hospitals where they'll inject her, wipe her down, and patch her up good as new.

Maybe if she'd been looking up, adapting to the latest threats as the news advised, she might have seen the four figures that appeared to materialize from the alley.

Even when they are mere feet from her and her eyes finally reach them, it's hard to see the figures as more than impressions because, though Lisa insisted Carson was dark, 21st Street doesn't even have the neon and glow. She squints as the alley meets the street, turning the figures from Monet brushstrokes into something more like humans.

The tall one is shirtless, male by birth or by hormone blockers or some back-alley mastectomy—she'd heard about those . . . somewhere. His face is obscured by the shadow of the umbrella hat, but his evening-anchor white teeth shine with something dangling over the bottom row.

"Hewo dere, doggy." He reaches a long, sinewy arm down to Koko, the thing hanging from his tongue flapping on his chin. Was that a condom? Why? In this neighborhood, those belong on the sidewalk for residents to photograph and catalog in the South Side Down Low Facebook group. "Gif uth a kith."

An eruption of cackles from the other three figures. Lisa spins around, finding herself surrounded like the sacrifice of a coven.

The girl—to Lisa she's a girl, but the costumes make it difficult to tell, maybe that's the point, one of the points; there seem to be as many as a Seurat painting— approaches Koko. She'd be lost in the shadows if her light-eating attire wasn't interrupted by bright white at the knees and elbows, like protection when bowled over in roller derby, but flush to her sleeves and leggings. No padding, just surgical masks. To guard the joints from viral particles? To make a statement on the futility of self-protection, that no matter what you do, the big, bad world will still get you? Nothing will be OK when it all ends in dust? You may as well wear two-ply protection on your elbows, a helmet on your foot, go out at night with your dog when the news says women like you are getting their throats slit in dark alleys by kids like these. Or maybe she just had extras lying around and wanted to look as absurd as possible, turning herself into a human rayograph on the black streets.

The girl runs her hand down Koko's back, and the dog jerks around, snapping her jaws, launching spittle into the night.

"Holy shit!" the girl shrieks, yanking her hand away. Koko lurches toward her, Lisa just quick enough to pull the leash attached to the harness, the tenuous piece of nylon keeping the carnage at bay.

"Koko, stop that. You probably shouldn't be trying to pet her. I don't know what's got into her, but I should be bringing her home so she can calm down." Lisa's heart may be beating faster than Koko's.

"Yeah, yeah, go home, grandma," the girl in the misplaced masks taunts like a kid on a playground, as if the next words out of her mouth will involve rubber and glue or double-dog dares or whatever the kids say today. Probably something profane and violent. "You don't wanna be here when the kids are out."

"Boo!" The boy jumps in front of Lisa, shaking his head, the condom swinging like Koko's tongue on a hot day. Now, it stays in the dog's mouth, and all she shows are glistening incisors, sharpened to points.

Koko leaps at her antagonist, fangs gnashing air as the boy uses his teenage reflexes to jump away and the 70 pounds of angry, scared dog gain enough force to overcome Lisa's 140 or so pounds of resistance. The dog lunges again at the boy.

"Oh thit!" He breaks into a run. Koko copies, and Lisa, holding tight to the leash, becomes the third reluctant sprinter. What the boy's legs have in length they lack in speed, and his super-wide-leg jeans negate all the aerodynamics of his lack of a shirt. They eat up ground, but almost in slow motion. He's not an athlete, probably spends too much time on his phone, letting his muscles atrophy, even the figurative mental one becoming more and more dependent on the little device. Lisa's no athlete either—that kind of physical pursuit always seemed antithetical to the emotive, expressive aspects of abstract art—but she has to keep up with the dog, and adrenaline propels her toward Carson Street.

The fight-or-flight response. But isn't flight supposed to mean fleeing the predator, not running toward the danger? Can one really chase in self-defense? Apparently Koko thinks so. She barks at the boy, as he rounds the corner to Carson Street, a long, guttural sound that doesn't so much end as fade into a growl.

"Koko, stop." Lisa tugs on the leash, but she's lost all power, all control. First to the kids, succumbing to their terror tactics, staying off the streets at night as they clearly want those old enough to remember terror attacks to do. Now to her pet. Dog bites man, man bites dog, dog walks owner.

They run past a bank closed for the weekend, a vintage boutique closed for the night, a day spa closed forever. Lisa doesn't need to look up to know where they are. She knows this neighborhood enough to know few of the sidewalk slabs are aligned. A trip and the dog would drag owner over cracked pavement ripping through her jeans, friction burns on the few areas of pale flesh not pierced by shattered glass. Her body would open to the detritus of the sidewalk, trading her blood for filth and excrement. Blood spilled on the sidewalk. Do they smell it? Would they come running, drawn to the open vein, those bloodthirsty killers in Akron, Louisville, Chicago?

She keeps her eyes down as the dog pulls her past a vape shop that casts a green glow on the sidewalk and a pizza joint and its tumbling sandwich board—no match for a charging pit bull mix. A sudden turn, and the sidewalk turns to black tiles.

A half-dressed teenager, an artist, and a dog run into a bar.

The boy's legs slide on the slick floor past a pool table in the back of the near-empty Bat Cave bar, bursting through the saloon doors into a sleek, metal kitchen.

Lisa skids to a halt as Koko collides with a pair of legs. They're clad in loose denim and attached to a hefty Latino dressed for a barrio turf war, which may be appropriate for the South Side this evening.

"You gotta calm your dog down or you can't be here. And you three—you got ID?"

Lisa turns back to the doorway, sees the girls behind her, daring to edge past her to face a growling Koko.

"We're not trying to come into this sus joint," the one in spandex biker shorts and black T-shirt embellished with beads and shoulder pads says. The moderate light of the bar reveals eye makeup that's part Alice Cooper, part Divine.

"And bullshit you need ID. You let our friend in," the masked one spits between heavy breaths.

"You mean this idiot?" A man in black pushes the boy past the pool table to the bar's service entrance.

"Always gotta be our hero." The bartender smiles, shakes his head, and crosses his Henri Rousseau-style tattooed arms across his chest.

"I dunno. Idiot apprehension's not that hard." The man, his ink sleeves as faded as a van Gogh over time, pushes the kid around the bar until he reaches the blockade. Koko snarls.

"Koko, calm down. It's OK. He can't hurt you now." Lisa kneels on the floor, hugs her dog as she would in a thunderstorm, and feels both their hearts racing almost in unison.

"You got Straub?" Lisa hears her voice saying. Does she want that? Does it matter?

Hank, the man in black, yanks the kid, the condom still flapping on his tongue, around the bar. As they push past, Koko rises again to her haunches.

"C'mon, Koko, it's OK now." Lisa pats the dog on her back, pulls the leash, and for the first time since they encountered the kids, Koko obeys. Lisa takes a seat on one of the stools, its red cushion intact, legs even, unlike the rocking experience to which she's grown accustomed at Jake's. Koko settles in on the floor, leaning against her owner's leg.

"Oh, so you let a dog in and not us?!" the third girl in the ripped Nirvana T-shirt shrieks.

"She's old enough in dog years." The bouncer pushes the kids from the threshold. He kicks the stopper, and the door shuts. "Now I get why everyone else has these closed."

The bartender slides a pint to Lisa. She sips. It doesn't have that lotion taste that she's come to accept at Jake's Mistake. This draft is crisp, refreshing, and she knows that one sip doesn't alter her brain, but she feels the 4.1 percent ABV wash over her, and she's emerging a Venus from a seashell.

THEY DRINK OUR BLOOD

Hank reclaims his seat three stools down, marked with the half-empty rocks glass, the only other patron in this quiet bar.

"Your dog need one, too?" the bartender asks.

"No, she's OK. I've never given her any beer, though I know she's had paint water before. It's OK, cause I mostly use acrylics nowadays. But yeah, she's much better now. I've never seen her like that before. She was being her normal, sweet, curious self when those kids showed up and she just freaked."

"Maybe they're vampires," Hank says, putting the glass to his thin lips.

The bartender laughs. Hank grins.

"Vampires?" Lisa turns to Hank. "What makes you say that?"

"Dogs hate vampires. At least that's what old lore says. You never read vampire lore?"

"No, I'm not much a fan of scary things. I like things pretty, and I don't read a lot anyway."

"You watch the news?"

"Yes."

"Well, the news will have you believe we're living in a horror movie."

"And the kids, they could be the vampires?"

"He's just messing with you," the bartender says.

"But really, that would explain a lot, wouldn't it?" Lisa says. "It's all connected. The kids are just a disguise for the vampires. So maybe it wasn't a kid fleeing the alley in Nashville. Maybe it was a vampire that just looks young, dressed like a teenager. It'd explain the kids running amok in all these cities where people are getting their heads near torn off."

"Well, sure. Vampires can explain anything you can't," Hank says. "Rabies. Vitamin deficiencies. Genetic disorders. Everyone assumes we're living at the culmination of science. Maybe the provincial folk in the days before we figured out an all-corn diet may cause you to get pale and die thought they did, too. People never really change. Maybe a person, but not people. They commit the same fallacies over and over in every generation. So right now, you've got a generation of assholes. No one can—or wants to—explain 'cause maybe that means they're to blame, so the old vampire pops up again. Anything we can't figure out must be vampires. Not a thought that maybe we're just not that smart yet. We're certainly not. We're just like 19th- century Romanian peasants.

"It's not always vampires."

"I get what you're saying," Lisa says, placing her glass back on the bar. "Really, I do. I get that there'll probably be some boring explanation for everything supernatural in the future—"

"Wouldn't that be depressing?" The bartender mindlessly runs a rag over the black, polished bar, maybe in the hope he'll set more drinks on it this evening.

"I don't know how else to explain all these things I've seen with my own eyes. Koko here trying to protect me from those kids. Last night nearly getting caught in that mob. Seeing a woman, neck all torn up and bloody after they passed through. Then you got Emily down in Nashville. Louisville—"

"Now they're saying some unsolved murder in New Orleans is similar," the bartender says.

"See?" Lisa kicks for emphasis. Koko yelps. "Sorry, girl. I just got all excited." Then, to the other humans, "See, that's not a coincidence."

"No, but would you have thought vampires if the news didn't suggest it?" Hank asks.

"I don't ever think vampires. So probably not."

"There you go. You gotta remember they're just trying to entertain you between commercial breaks."

Above the bar, faces in evolving zombie makeup stare down at her. Framed 8x10 glossies with signatures in the corners. Even those who avoid horror movies know the city's rich genre history. She's in the right place for answers when she's living in one.

"So, let's say there are such things as vampires. How do you check?"

"Well, you could shove garlic in their faces," Hank says. "If they turn away, they could be vampires. Or just normal people who don't like strangers assaulting them with allium. People doing the low-FODMAP thing."

"They don't have reflections," the bartender says.

"Why not?" Lisa asks.

"I think because they don't have souls."

"Neither do crypto bros, but that doesn't stop them from ogling themselves in mirrors."

This comment makes Hank laugh.

"What else?"

"You could wave a crucifix at them. Spray them with holy water."

"I don't have any of that on me."

"Well, it's a good thing you have your dog."

Aside from the tugs on the leash when the dog is distracted by a scent only she can smell, Lisa lets Koko guide her home. The dog is her protector. Not from vampires. Like the guys at the bar said, believing the cause of your worries is vampires is what silly or illiterate people did throughout history. Lisa is college educated, in art, not science, but still she took the required courses. She doesn't watch the haunting shows. She understands that an orb captured on camera is a trick of the light. She does know her zodiac sign, Pisces, because she was a teenage girl once, too. But what does it mean to be born under a fish? Nothing to Lisa.

It's silly, and Lisa isn't a peasant, but she's also not one to deny a truth just because she may not have witnessed it firsthand. Didn't all those stories over centuries that Hank called lore amount to something? Maybe they didn't commit all the crimes for which they were blamed—yes, some people were consumptive, not undead— but that doesn't rule out their existence. And, after all, the national news mentioned the possibility.

Her vigilance, enhanced by the brush with immortal evil, supernatural or not, doesn't keep her from nearly colliding with the lanky figure emerging from the shadows of the intersecting alley.

"My lady. I didn't mean to startle you like that."

His face may as well be hidden behind a René Magritte apple, because it blends into the darkness. The dapper, anachronistic bowler hat and tailored gray suit would scream vampire if she didn't know him.

"Oh, hi Walter."

Koko sniffs the gray pants, shoves her snout into the long, spindly shin.

"No, it's OK. I'm just a little on edge. Some folks got me thinking Koko and I may have run into some vampires earlier, and I'm trying to square that with everything I know about the world. It has me doubting everything. And I don't believe in goblins or zombies or anything like that, but I can't stop thinking I ran into vampires right about here not even an hour ago tonight, and I don't—"

"Why do you think such creatures don't exist?"

"There's no proof, I guess."

"I've known vampires are real for a long time. Government used to pay me to infiltrate their underworld and all that. I seen vampires in three-piece suits with wings on their backs swooping into a parlor and fooling the young ladies thinking they were coming in for an innocent kiss."

Over the years, Lisa has heard enough from Walter on his barstool at Jake's Mistake, and its previous incarnation as Ledbetter's, to doubt he was any more a government agent than Walter Sickert was Jack the Ripper, but there's something comforting about another person who just might believe. Someone, even an eccentric old barfly who dresses like the *Son of Man,* understands.

"So, if the government knows, why are there all these vampires now?"

"Same as always. Vampires have money. They've been around forever, wandering from place to place, collecting from their victims, using their ill-gotten wealth to hide in plain sight. Meanwhile, they suck blood. That's why the government had me watching 'em. Make sure they don't get too out of hand. Stay hidden. Looks like someone messed up. Maybe they'll pull me out of retirement."

Walter tips his hat as Lisa lets Koko pull her in the direction of home. Was Walter right? Have vampires always been here, in some sort of tacit don't-ask-don't-tell agreement with the government? It sounded a little conspiratorial, but Lisa can't deny what she saw when she and Koko had walked in the opposite direction. The dog sensed evil in those kids and jumped to defend her. Animal instinct from a species that still has to fight for survival from lower on the food chain than humans at the top. Or are we? When will we be usurped by something stronger, smarter? When will we finally have a predator? Lisa doesn't watch the alien shows either, has never seen any evidence this threat will come from outer space.

If you watch the news, hear the testimonials of her neighbors, witness a stampede that left an aspiring nurse bleeding from the jugular, you have evidence of the threat coming from within: The kids are evil.

And they need adults to clean up after them.

So as soon as day breaks, or maybe a few hours after dawn as when Lisa arrived, the members of the SNAC—the South Side Neighborhood Action Committee—and the neighbors who made good on their enthused comments under the South Side Down Low post are gathering trash into bags on Carson Street. It's the South Side's main drag, but with the historic buildings occupied by decidedly unhistoric neon Kratom signs, it could be the nightlife neighborhood of any city: Baltimore, Louisville, Chicago, Akron, Nashville.

The habitual do-gooders come equipped with their pointed sticks while the rest of the 20 or so concerned citizens are testing their endurance at bending and straightening.

For the second time in 12 hours, Lisa considers joining a group class at the fitness studio two doors down from Jake's where she peers through the window to see women in yoga pants lifting little dumbbells with a frequency that likely exceeds Lisa's lifting of brush to canvas or even pint to mouth. But then she considers the camaraderie and its antithetical relationship to the solitary life of the artist.

Sure, there are community movements. Even cubism was a product of two minds. But when Lisa decided art was her calling back in middle school, in the back of her mind she knew it was partly because it was something she could pursue with no interference.

Then why is she here? Why has she suddenly forsaken her canvases to spend her evenings in the company of strangers? Online, at the bar, or in her car—all at the expense of the lonely, incomplete orange squares? Is it because here there is no Lisa? Here, she is 1/38th of a group, no expectation to be a whole. She's a part of something bigger than she now understands her squares never could be.

"Lisa?"

She shoves a Monster Energy can into her trash bag, stands up, her sacroiliac joint screaming like a teenager with surgical masks on her elbows.

"Oh, hi Marc."

"It's so great to see you!" Marc says, arms open. Lisa drops the bag and leans in for a light hug, European style. "This is my partner, Lee."

Marc motions to what may be his blond twin, same lean six feet, tapered pants in varying colors of Monet's water lilies depending on the position of the sun, white polo shirts. Lee smiles, shrugs, giggles, and hugs her, too.

"Lee, Lisa worked at the Amadeo Gallery next door to the office."

"Oh! Did you teach the paint-your-pet class?" Lee asks.

"I taught a bunch of those. Paint your pet. Paint your spouse. Paint your mom. Paint your house. Paint your—"

"Yes! We loved that. Still have both our paintings of Franny over the mantel. Mine's better." Lee winks.

"Lisa's an artist." Marc turns to his partner. "She doesn't think either of our renditions of Franny is Berthe Morisot's greyhound."

"I'm sure they're both lovely." Lisa smiles the way she used to at the gallery, the expression unfamiliar in the past six months. "And you can capture the spirit of your pet regardless of technical skill."

"You're a darling, Lisa. But you're lying," Marc taps her arm. "Lisa paints these shapes—all different colors, textures."

"Shapes?"

"Squares mostly. Some circles."

"And trapezoids." Marc raises his arm in emphasis, and milk foam cascades over the rim of his cup. Lee shakes his head, and Marc shakes the sticky liquid from his hand. "I swear I remember trapezoids."

"That was probably when I got sloppy."

"Are you showing anywhere else soon? I was so sad about Amadeo's."

"Not now. I actually haven't been painting much recently."

"What?" Marc claps his empty hand over his comically dropped jaw. "That's sacrilege. Why not?"

Lisa looks into Marc's gray eyes, but when she starts to speak, her gaze is unfocused, as if she's staring into an abyss.

"I've been an artist my entire life, and I guess it's been because I loved to do it. The physical act of painting. I could get lost in it. I once heard some quote from someone that painting could make him forget about the war, and it was like that with me. Ever since I was a kid. Hours would go by, and I hadn't realized. It wouldn't matter what I was painting. So I went to art school for it and kept getting lost in it. And no, it doesn't matter what I mean by my art but what the viewer experiences from it, like Camille said when she pretended my art was important."

Marc opens his mouth to interject, likely with platitudes: *No, your art is important. All art is important. It meant something to me when I saw it. I mean, not enough to buy it, I guess, but to see it on the wall when I'd stop by to chat with Camille after picking up a latte.*

None of these words come out before Lisa continues: "But it's not. It's a damn trapezoid when I tried to make a square. There's no meaning. It's just a way for the artist to zone out and avoid what's important. To pretend I'm contributing. But I wasn't. I was just doing what I wanted to do. Selfish. Only a few of us can paint works that change people's minds or open up a new way of perceiving the world or spurring an experience so emotional it borders on religious. The rest of us paint so when an interior decorator picks us off a gallery wall because we match a sofa, some rich guy won't be offended. We get out of school thinking we're gonna be the one that changes the world, but we get into the world and hide from it in our studios when we realize no one with money pays people who want to change society because that means they won't be the ones with the money anymore, and real quick we just try to become Thomas Kinkade.

"We create pretty things, not art. And we become OK with that because it means we can keep painting our hours away because it's what we love to do. And who does it serve? The stockbroker in the high-rise who wanted a conversation piece at cocktail parties? To pretend finance guys have some depth? He's not worried he's gonna lose his bar because of crazy kids running around acting like vampires. So I'm helping some white-collar criminal impress his clients while my own neighborhood is burning? What's the purpose of art if that's all it does? What's the purpose of an artist now, when you turn on the news and everyone else except that rich guy needs help? And I know I can't help them all. I know that. But I can do this. I can come down here because they may not need me as an artist right now, but they need me to be part of this operation, and I'm here to help." And when she finally verbalizes it, she understands the ennui of the past six months.

A second of silence before Marc opens his mouth. "Well, I'm so glad you're here to help! The neighborhood needs all it can get."

THEY DRINK OUR BLOOD

"Now more than ever." Lee nods with that look that says empathy so clearly; he never needs to bend down and pick up trash. He knows. He understands. He and Marc walk away, lattes in hand, the hot, tan liquid threatening to erupt again over the lid-free rims.

Lisa tosses a crumpled Ollipop can into the trash bag that she drags around the corner to three red splotches on the sidewalk. Lisa could jump to conclusions and assume she's stumbled upon the scene of another attack. She can hypothesize, but to assume, she'll need more information.

She snaps a photo, capturing the splotches and their accompanying splatters in their loose formation like a Jackson Pollock rendition of China's flag. "Corner of Carson and 20th. Anyone know what happened?" She types then hits "post," and the photo uploads to the group. She closes Facebook, stares at the mess on the ground that lesser abstract expressionists on Instagram attempt to emulate with randomness. Has a minute passed? She opens Facebook, taps the notifications.

The first comment has no words, just an animated Bela Lugosi head.

"For all you guys saying vampires were bullshit," the next comment reads. Lisa clicks the link below it.

The headline of the story, linking to local TV station WTF News, reads *Denning vs. Dracula? Actor reports vampire attack.*

The video at the top of the linked page autoplays an ad for the station's illustrious, award-winning, acclaimed, trusted, deified weather team. When an ad for a local car dealership follows, Lisa scrolls down to the teleprompter words transcribed on the page.

Actor Ty Denning claims he was attacked by a vampire early Sunday morning in the city's South Side. At around 2:45 a.m., said college student Chad Kerch, 21, he was walking down one of the neighborhood's many alley-like streets when he saw a man on the ground and another kneeling over him, sucking the blood from the victim's neck.

"I didn't know it was a famous actor, just saw this dude on the ground with this other creepy dude biting his neck," Kerch said. "First I thought it was just two dudes getting it on and, like, you know, but then it really looked like the dude on the ground was in pain and it was like, nonconsensual."

Kerch says as he approached the two men, the "vampire" took off with "crazy speed down the alley and disappeared into the darkness like he turned into a bat or something." The Duquesne senior credits his bicep Celtic cross tattoo for "scaring off the vampire."

Denning was taken to an area hospital, where he is listed in good condition.

Lisa attempts to scroll for more when a succession of pop-up ads floods the screen, swallowing the story, engulfing the words in a tsunami of animations so aggressive their escape from the virtual into the physical realm seems imminent.

Dragging her thumb from the bottom of the screen closes Facebook and everything that comes with it. But what of Lisa's post? What of the blood on the sidewalk? Surely it's related to the attack?

She reopens the app to find, as is so often the case of the ones who ask questions by those who demand action, her post buried by the words: Stop the violence! Community meeting at Saint Odessa Church, 7 p.m.

To Lisa, Saint Odessa is less a place of worship than an event hall. That's what sent her into churches in the decades earlier in her life: funerals and weddings. Churches were places to commemorate death or celebrate life. The speeches and readings from some ancient book meant nothing more than time to examine the magnificent architecture, the play of light as it refracted through the stained glass, the triptych behind the altar.

The organizers moved the community meeting into the chapel from the regular area in the basement because of unanticipated high turnout and a shortage of chairs. So Lisa sits in a pew, and she thinks it's safer anyway, what with the preponderance of crucifixes. For those to whom church is a solemn affair, the speakers taking their turns behind the dais lend divine veritas to their pleas for increased police presence. To the cynics, it adds an element of hysteria, as if the speakers are not requesting allocation of municipal funds but for the Lord to smite the miscreants. God, send a mighty deluge to wipe out this hell-spawned plague from our righteous, bar-lined streets. Grant us our hedonistic vices of lust and indulgence; just eradicate the violence. Smite them with extreme prejudice, O holy one!

THEY DRINK OUR BLOOD

The words circle her head in the enormous room like spirits, so close to possessing her with the ideas of her neighbors but never quite penetrating. At least, not when Lisa's head is in the art of this Catholic church. Art is expression, capable of connecting disparate populations through the universal language of the human experience. No matter who you are, you can extract meaning. As Camille would say, even from squares.

Some people don't know the difference between a Mondrian and a bathroom tile.

Others don't understand religious iconography or local politics. And find them both equally boring.

The words float beneath the flying buttresses and the rest of the architectural features Lisa can name more accurately than any of the saints.

Police presence.

Curfew.

Traffic restrictions.

She looks to the wooden Jesus, his tortured expression, the pain in his eyes that conveys a peace with the world as if to say, "Don't cry for me. I get it. Do better next time," carved onto a wooden cross.

Who has to die for there to be some action around here?

Stay home.

Proactive policing.

If you see something, say something.

The same recycled advice to ward off anything from a virus to a bomb. It echoes under the vaulted ceilings, ricocheting off the stained-glass windows, swirling through the pews until it becomes the echo of an echo of an echo, back to the pleading eyes of the dead Jew on the cross. Among all the medieval-style art, all wearing the same angelic visage as if sin can be airbrushed away, Jesus with his gaunt cheeks and gaping mouth and those eyes, those goddamn eyes, knows what it means to be human. And Lisa can't look away.

So many words, meaningless filler, classic all-talk, no-action yet infused with gravitas due to the setting.

Community policing.

Neighborhood first.

Public messaging.

Responsible bar ownership.

Bouncer training.

All these words floating from apse to narthex. And yet one word, the only important word, the word that Lisa thinks is on the tip of everyone's tongue, has yet to be spoken.

"We'll now be seeking comments from the community." The speaker is all but hidden behind the rostrum fitted for a priest presumably taller than Mary Wintrove, who, Lisa just learned, in 40 years of service is the longest-tenured, though shortest in stature, board member. "We have a bigger group than usual, hence the change in venue, so please be patient."

"Yes, I'd like to say something." Lisa's voice quavers as she rises from her pew. All the eyes—there must be hundreds of pairs in here, a full Mass worth—staring at the one who dares to stand. While they're dressed in their Sunday worst, is the act of obedient listening still ingrained in them from a childhood spent in places like this? Are they still as reverent of the icons above the altar as Lisa is to hers on the walls of the MOMA?

"OK, you first," comes the disembodied voice of Mary Wintrove.

"I'm just wondering—"

"Speak up!" Wintrove commands. Easy for the old lady with the microphone.

Lisa summons the air from deep in her diaphragm to make her voice heard over even the most enthusiastic bachelorette party, ostensibly celebrating a new chapter while apparently trying to relive their youth in one of her painting classes at the gallery, drinking cheap wine and singing along to Lauryn Hill.

"I'm wondering if anyone has any ideas of things we can actually do."

A snort from somewhere in the pews, packed like a wedding for a couple that fell somewhere between sitting on homecoming court and being relegated to eating lunch in a bathroom stall.

Lisa continues: "So far, everyone's talking about the mayor doing a walk-through and getting police patrols and off-duty cops moonlighting, but none of that is anything those of us in this room can do. We heard Mike say his bar's in danger, and Jake's Mistake isn't the only one. I was in the Bat Cave last night, and I was one of only two customers, three if you count my dog, but they didn't charge her for water so she wasn't really a customer. And that's a Saturday night! It's dire, right? We let our 21-and-over bars go under, and what's left here for us? They just take over. It's all good to get the city council involved, but how will that protect us when we walk home from here tonight? I know it started early, but it'll still be sundown when we leave, and how will we protect ourselves and our community?"

"It sounds like you have ideas for action. Would you like to share them?"

"Well, this is a church, isn't it?" Lisa's voice shakes again. "There's gotta be some holy water around here somewhere."

The only laughter Lisa had ever heard in church was the polite titter when a priest attempted to infuse some local sports humor into a lengthy, tedious wedding Mass. This is a cacophony of guffaws, yelps, scoffs usually reserved, in this space, for a nonbeliever. Yet, it's peppered with, "Shut up; that's what we're all thinking!" and "I don't hear a better idea!"

"A serious idea," Mary says.

"This is serious." Her voice is finally steady, like back in a college critique, the nerves worn off after the painting is presented to the class. It's out there now, and there's nothing Lisa can do other than defend it. "Have you seen what's on the streets? My dog knows. She senses something's wrong."

"Well, by all means, if your dog has psychic powers . . . "

"My dog can sense a vampire better than any human can. She's got no preconceived notions or judgment, doesn't second-guess herself, hasn't read any science books explaining away all those hundreds of years of tales about the dead rising and drinking our blood. She smells something wrong when she's around those kids, doesn't even know the word 'vampire,' just knows it's evil."

Muttering. Tsks.

"My dog hates teenagers, too."

"I cannot believe this is happening."

"Best time I've had in church since ever."

"Only in South Side."

"I mean, why not, with all the body of Christ talk in this place, it kinda makes sense."

"OK, moving along." Mary is rolling her eyes, just above the rostrum. "Next comment."

Lisa falls back in her pew as something about illuminating backstreets garners a round of semi-enthusiastic "yeahs" from the nave.

Stop signs.

Speed humps.

As if traffic is the imminent threat. Long-term grievances likely aired at every opportunity no matter how irrelevant to the matter at hand: bloodsuckers. Fiends. The dark ones that lurk in the shadows.

Aside from some residents of the poorly lit backstreets volunteering to invest in solar lights for their stoops—just $12 for Amazon Prime members—the action Lisa requested is still wanting when all rise from their pews and shuffle into the aisle. As she ambles into the crowd, a whiff transports her to a bar. There's no need to describe the smell to anyone who's ever been in a dive before smoking bans. It's an anachronism, nostalgic for those who drank their memories rosy when nights were anything but.

A hot, humid cloud of stale lager wets her ear. She wishes she'd cut it off. "You know, you're right. We gotta do something."

Lisa turns, opens her mouth to say she'll be getting to work as soon as she gets out of this room, but Jake's owner Mike has already begun pushing his way toward the narthex and the doors he must have forgotten are locked.

A staple remover was never on the supply list for any of Lisa's art courses. Staple gun, yes. Remover, no. That's because usually when an artist staples a canvas to its wooden stretchers, the artist, unless also a framer, does not remove the finished piece from the frame. And, unlike the often exacting process of painting in which errors are covered by layers of oil, entire compositions hidden under superior final drafts, canvas-stretching mishaps are easily mitigated by adding, not subtracting, staples. And a run-of-the-mill office-supply staple remover is not strong enough to extract the construction-grade metal staples from wood.

That's a job for Lisa's chisel, which was on the supply list for Sculpture II junior year. Subtractive art, yes, but for plaster, not deconstructing a painting. It was supposed to create.

At one of the five salvaged tables in her studio, Lisa wedges the angled tip under the staple, pulling just enough to provide clearance to pry it free. Her hand is aching after seven repetitions when she places the loose canvas—a vignette-surrounded orange square in the creases of years stretched around its square frame within the frayed, square cloth, three concentric squares—atop the stack of dismantled canvases. She stretches her fingers, as she has after every successful canvas extraction, fighting off the claw her overused right hand wants to become. Even in deconstructing her art, she's lost track of time.

Junior year in high school is that odd filler time when most of the basic lessons of art are taught before the higher concepts of the two-hour college-level course availed to students like Lisa as seniors. It was also when her teacher—a lively brunette, not ancient by high school standards, could have been 23 or 40, young enough to impart lessons that may resonate with the students—recounted a story. All Lisa can recall of the setting is a classroom with paint-speckled four-person tables and art hanging in the few free spaces on the walls: the highest honor to which a student could aspire. Her fellow students and all chronological context are a Gaussian blur. The monologue from this teacher, who is now nothing more than a hair color and a generation, are lost to decades of other memorable turns of phrase, but the message is one Lisa will never forget.

This teacher was about her students' age in an art class much like the one Lisa was in when her teacher took a knife to all the students' work. She slashed canvases, smashed hardened clay, and ripped drawings with such ferocity the charcoal exploded in a Lebron James chalk cloud. It wasn't jealousy, the students surpassing the teacher; it was a lesson. Your work is not precious. Anything can be destroyed. Klimt, van Gogh, Klee, Schiele, Courbet, Raphael: All had works destroyed by Nazis. You are not your art. You cannot cling to your past creations. You will always have to make something new. Evolve. Adapt. Do not rest on what you once did. That is not art. That is production.

Even for 16-year-old Lisa, the story struck her as apocryphal. This didn't happen to her teacher. It was just a story repeated across generations of art teachers to their students, some of whom would become teachers and keep the legend alive. And every aspiring artist would understand anything could be disposable, and they would never stop creating, and they would always know they weren't their art. So, even if the particular narrative and the characters were invented somewhere in the chain, the story itself was real. Fact and fiction are not mutually exclusive.

Lisa pulls the wooden canvas stretcher bars apart at their tongue-and-groove connections. She sets two on the table and crosses the remaining two at a 90-degree angle. Using her glue gun—a relic from Sculpture I—she adheres them where they meet. Lisa removes a canvas from the pile, the orange square with its purple stroke seamlessly becoming the black background thick with impasto application but not so thick as to make it impenetrable by X-Acto knife. She makes four slits in the canvas. It's still pliable enough to wrap around the stretcher bar cross, pull taut, and staple the excess in the back.

In its original form, before this stretcher reassignment surgery, it was to be a gift for a wedding—if only she'd received an invitation—a potential Christmas present for a college friend if she'd stayed in touch, a birthday surprise for Aunt Carol if she'd just kept up her biweekly calls before the cancer. Maybe being an artist who gave her own work as gifts was the reason she was gradually deleted from the invitation lists. Not that she ever had the chance to give as many paintings as she'd created, but those three times may have appeared to be a pattern.

There's something off-putting about a professional artist giving her work away at every occasion. Overvaluing its worth to the potential recipients as if it supersedes items on the registry while simultaneously undervaluing it by reducing the price to free and saturating the market. Abundance is not a selling point unless you're Warhol and you've turned the banality of mass production into art. So now, Lisa finds herself with a glut of squares to spare, worthless . . . at least in their original geometry . . .

But in another shape, a cross, she has enough for her entire community, and *that* has value. Real utilitarian value. No eye of the beholder. An aesthetic that could be displayed in even the most godless parts of town. The Edvard Munch colors would look right at home next to the signed frame from local George Romero vampire classic *Martin* on the Bat Cave wall.

Lisa is a step ahead of the news. Upon returning from the community meeting and its decisive lack of action, she Googled ways to ward off a vampire. She's already created her first cross when the expert, a professor of folklore at some college—Lisa didn't catch the name—is just getting to undead defense. In the evening national broadcast that's been playing on the TV at her periphery, the professor has made it clear he's not citing illiterate-peasant rumors when he presents his first recommendation.

"Silver bullets," the professor says.

"Wait—I thought those were for werewolves," the newscaster through her surgically plumped lips interrupts. These people with money and a job that pays for physical appearance can be just as ambiguous in age as vampires, Lisa thinks.

"That's the thing about vampires. There's so many incarnations in so many cultures, you could find an aegis in any one of them."

"So I can go after them with, say, a bottle of pepper spray? A Taser?"

"I doubt that. Most vampire legends end before the industrial revolution. Enlightenment, the scientific method, evidence, less reliance on religion and superstition: Those are the biggest vampire killers."

"So what are the most common weapons? The ones shared by a plurality of cultures?"

"Well, to repel vampires, a cross, a crucifix, any religious object really."

"From any religion?"

"Most commonly Christianity, but everyone from Jews to the Zoroastrians has demon-type creatures that drain their victims of their life force in some capacity. But I think the vampires we are discussing here are of the type more likely to fear a cross than, say, a mezuzah."

Lisa smiles at her creations, now a stack of three. She's on the right track.

The well-fed expert with the graying beard continues, "Holy water is believed to cause burns but isn't lethal. Of course, that would be a good way to weaken them for when you inflict the fatal blow."

"Which is?"

"Well, there again the legends vary. But a stake through the heart usually does it."

"Usually?"

"You could always chop off the head to be sure."

"OK, but if you're going to start beheading, you should probably be sure—"

"To be sure, yes, and that's the tragedy of so many of these stories. Graves dug up. Corpses exhumed. Loved ones traumatized. Even innocents murdered—usually as scapegoats for a deadly contagion."

"What did they claim made one a vampire?"

"Historically, like I said about the graves, people believed the recently deceased were actually undead and had escaped their tombs at night to feed on their living relations. Supposed disturbances in the dirt by the tombstone and moribund family members usually cast suspicions on a culprit who couldn't defend him or herself: a dead person. And when the body was exhumed, suspicions would be confirmed when the nails and hair appeared to have grown, which we know now to be nothing more than the natural process of skin retracting as the corpse dehydrates. And blood around the mouth, which is—"

"But what about vampires that have traveled and aren't going after just family?"

"You mean like Dracula crossing the sea to England?"

"Sure."

"That type of vampire is the product of our modern folklore: literature. Those are the vampires that don't have a reflection. They're nocturnal and may present as anachronisms due to the bygone era in which they truly lived."

"So maybe they're dressed from a different era?"

"Maybe."

A different era. Like a teenager wearing JNCO jeans 30 years late? Maybe those kids weren't mocking their parents. Maybe they were their parents, or the age they would have been in the' 90s when those clothes were fashionable. Maybe they were stuck in a state of arrested development, eternal adolescence, damned to forever feed off the adults. Invincible and awkward. Maybe the decades without change made them accustomed to their bodies, not like the rest of us in a constant state of flux. For a second, Lisa pities them, the emotional turmoil of a day in the life of a 16-year-old. Are they tormented like that forever, spending their angst-ridden waking hours in a quest for blood?

"They also don't appear in mirrors or photographs—"

"Which is why it's so hard to prove their existence?" the newscaster interjects.

"Uh, among other reasons. I was going to say, vampire legend has not evolved with technology. There's nothing in the folklore claiming vampires don't appear in moving images—in film or digital."

"So we may be able to see vampires in, say, a TikTok video?"

"As I explain in my book—"

"Excuse me, Dr. Modigliani, I'm just getting word we have breaking news."

The bearded half of the screen disappears. Lonnie is alone just long enough to say, "Mia Reeve is on the ground with our sister station in Ithaca, New York, with the story; Mia?" before she's replaced by another blonde, maybe a decade younger, the age when she still gets stuck with standing-in-the-dark-rain assignments, before she slides into Lonnie's time slot and no one notices the difference. Generations of blondes all morphed into one, like a TV vampire.

"Thank you, Lonnie. I'm here on the Cornell campus outside the building housing the English department from which police have just removed a body. We are told the deceased is a professor from the university. He was found dead in his office. Now, the reason police have declared this a crime scene is because the coroner observed two puncture wounds about an inch apart—what I'm told is fang distance—on the neck. Aside from a smidgen of blood around the wound—right on a major artery—there was no blood elsewhere on the victim or in the office.

THEY DRINK OUR BLOOD

"I'm told this suggests he's been drained of blood. We do not have an ID on the victim yet as the family is still being notified, but we will keep you updated when that information is available. Till then, this is Mia Reeve with Channel 6 evening news."

Back in the main studio, Lonnie recaps the story to the middle-aged sports reporter. It's out of hand. Existential threats. It's hard for Lisa to make out more words over the clatter as she tosses paintbrushes, palette knives, compasses, and rulers to the cement floor until from deep in her supply bin, she pulls out her saw. It's small: just a handsaw, no motor. The blade is thin, flimsy, and likely dull.

She stands at her table, leaning all her weight on the canvas stretcher to keep it in place as she saws back and forth. Sweat dripping from her forehead, she finally severs the end at about a 30-degree angle, leaving a sharp tip. It's not smooth—jagged and possibly sharper than the saw blade—but she won't be the one taking it through the heart, so what does she care if it leaves splinters? What's a splinter going to do when a creature is dying for the second time?

And any vampire would know what it meant before Lisa would even have to think about stabbing it into the horrid fiend's chest.

Sonia's expression says she'd be woefully unprepared when encountering a vampire. It's a good thing her neighbor stopped by. Jejune Sonia, apparently never pranked with a flaming bag of crap, may never entertain the notion that a knock on her door could be anything more ominous than a Jehovah's Witness. If her buzzer rang, it was a delivery, a present given by herself or someone who's thinking of her. As now, when Lisa comes bearing gifts.

"Oh hey, Lisa. I've got your oil. Come in, let me get it for—is that my doormat?"

"You can't leave it out here. I've been reading up on it. 'Welcome' is an invitation to a vampire. You don't need to be formal; they're not Dracula. They're contemporary, and they respond to contemporary things. Some people are even saying a head tilt and a door opening is enough. Like if you even just let go of the chain and don't act like you're about to slam the door in their faces, they'll just come in."

Lisa shoves the gritty mat at the younger artist. Sonia hesitates, examining the debris between the rugged tufts. She watches the dust dissipate, maybe weighs the trouble of moving foot dirt into her studio living space against arguing with a manic neighbor and her insistent stare. Finally, she accepts the mat.

"Come in, and I'll grab the oil." Sonia pulls the door open, sets the mat down, careful not to let the shoe detritus become airborne. She motions to the cowboy boots, Birkenstocks, and slip-ons lined up against the wall. Lisa slides out of her knock-off Crocs.

Sonia moves to the left, parting the tie-dye sheets suspended from rope strung through a grommet to a hook on the 15-foot ceiling. Before the makeshift curtain swings back into place, Lisa spies a standing easel and three orderly folding tables covered in smaller tabletop easels, cups filled with brushes, spray cans, and palettes.

Where Lisa stands by the door, it's a living space. A couch next to the shoes, in front of it a coffee table—half-eaten bowl of ramen noodles with edamame and Kurt Vonnegut's *Bluebeard* in the center. On the adjoining wall, shelves of books and records are interrupted by tropical plants. The kitchenette is in the back corner, the tucked-in queen bed closest to the enclosed work area.

It never occurred to Lisa to section off her studio from her living space. Her life was her art, a lesson from her teacher's story she chose to ignore.

"Your place is really nice," Lisa says as Sonia emerges from behind the sheet with the small bottle. "You shouldn't just let me in like that, though. I know we're neighbors and all, but you don't know I haven't been turned. There's no security in this building, and no one even got any of those video doorbells. That's why I brought you this."

"Is that . . . ? Lisa, is that one of your paintings?"

And Lisa is concerned that Sonia appears more concerned by the canvas wrapped into a cross than she was at the prospect of a vampire at her door.

"Yeah, it wasn't doing much good sitting around in my place. Now it has a purpose."

"You destroyed your own art?"

"What was the point of it just sitting around? It's not helping keep the community safe, not helping keep the neighborhood bars open. Now they can."

"They? Lisa, how many paintings did you . . . repurpose?"

"Seven so far, but I still have another 50 or so, maybe more, that I stripped out of their frames and will transform tonight. I'll be up late."

"So, like 60? Is that—"

"It's however many I had in my studio."

"Oh, Lisa, you destroyed your life's work. Who was that artist, the one that shattered all her sculptures?" Sonia blinks, lifts her knuckles to her forehead as if she's trying to press the art history lesson out.

"I didn't—" Lisa begins, but the art trivia has only been suppressed for the past six months, not the six years since Sonia's last college class, and the words flow out. "Oh, Claudel."

"Yes! And she was committed for paranoia, right? Died in an asylum?"

"But that was because her brother kept her there because they didn't believe in her career, and I don't have to worry about that because I'm not close to my family and they don't care that I chose this instead of, like, getting a traditional job or something like—"

"You're wrong about your art not helping anyone. That's what art does; it helps you understand something about yourself or the world you wouldn't have understood otherwise."

"It wasn't saving any lives."

"Maybe not like a vaccine or a Kevlar vest, but it makes you feel alive when you experience it." Sonia's pleading eyes appear to swell to the size of a Margaret Keane subject. Lisa lets hers drift to the easel and the bold, expressive, distorted view of the river from behind the flap of one of the many tents recently appearing on the trail. Maybe last year, she would have considered this painting some sort of comment on economic disparity, an attempt to put the bourgeois gallery visitor in the hovel of a ragamuffin, or a cynical comment on how illegal urban campers have the best views. Now, in the midst of a neighborhood siege, it's a distraction— beautiful, yet ultimately pointless.

Sonia's not ready to hear the harsh truth Lisa has finally discovered more than a decade and a half after she was her neighbor's age. She says, "So does doing my part to help."

Sonia nods, considering it for a moment. The earnestness bordering on desperation in Lisa's eyes finally persuades Sonia to accept the cross.

"What do I do with it?"

"Mount it on the wall. Close to the door. About eye level, so it's easy for you to reach in case a vampire attacks you. And just a couple of nails under each of its arms. Arms, right? I don't know what they're called. So you don't have a hard time taking it down. I'm happy to help you hang it. If you wait a sec, I'll be back with some nails."

"No need," Sonia says. "I don't want to inconvenience you like that. Besides, I have some nails here."

"It's not an inconvenience. I've only got one other project to do tonight."

"Then get on it! Seriously, I can do it myself."

"You sure? You gotta do it tonight, though."

Sonia's glance at the ramen on the table is not furtive enough. Lisa sees it, but who can think about food when a vampire wants your blood for dinner?

"I promise. Here." Sonia stuffs the cross under her arm, walks to the door, pulls it open with one hand and offers the little bottle of oil to Lisa with the other. Lisa accepts. She looks at the door like some lonely species who doesn't just need permission but needs to be forced to enter an empty hallway.

"OK." Lisa slides her feet into the shoes she refers to as Crocs. "But promise you'll hang it."

"You have my word."

One cross down. Fifty-nine to go.

When the afternoon sun shines through the warehouse windows and Koko's whines force the newly minted woodworker out of her slumber, it's not wooden stakes in demand for vampire defense.

It's silver.

Upon finally waking around 11 a.m., Lisa's first thought is the lack of blinds available for the industrial windows. Then she ambles to the couch and flicks on the TV.

Almost immediately, she learns that the American people choose glamour over violence. Fend off vampires and look good doing it with a silver chain around your tantalizing neck. Everyone has a bit of a *Saturn Devouring His Son* expression while stabbing. Face contoured, adrenaline pumping, taking over all other functions like sucking in a gut or keeping hair in place. And who actually knows how to stab? Most of us would be less Van Helsing, more Boomer trying a TikTok dance. A camera would capture an absurd pose, never meant to be seen in a still frame, something only possible in a cubist drawing.

No, it would be far easier to throw money at the problem. Buy silver.

Or not.

By the time Lisa is in the elevator with an impatient Koko and catches up on the conversation in the South Side Down Low, the local jeweler and three piercing shops on Carson have sold out of silver.

And apparently you want good silver.

The vampire experts of the late-night broadcasts failed to mention the nuances in silver as armor that the morning show experts explained in detail. Sterling silver is not good enough. The purer the silver, the more it burns the vampire. Alloys are ineffective—too diluted of the vampire-repelling power of the precious metal. It's not as though silver can kill a vampire anyway, just make the fiend uncomfortable, and like the religious objects, it's just a deterrent that can buy a savvy mortal some time.

While Koko sniffs the carcass of a Chinese lanternfly, Lisa Googles "Catholic shops Pittsburgh."

"If you're looking for a silver cross, we're sold out," the woman answers after one ring.

"What about other silver jewelry?"

"No. No rings, bracelets, anything."

"Do you have any charms made of silver at all? See, I'm an artist, and I already fashioned all these crosses out of canvas stretchers, and I can make anything you have into jewelry—"

"No. I'm sorry; we just sold our last piece this morning."

Phone in hand, Lisa lets Koko drag her over the potholes, along the alley at the back of her building. Does she really not own any good silver? Jewelry that's silver in color, yes, but the kind thinned with cheaper filler like a painting medium. A vampire would laugh with more condescension than those skeptics in the church last night, gnash its fangs into her neck, tearing out her esophagus, spitting out the cheap tin chain. That's all her jewelry is; chintzy trinkets she picked up to match an outfit when she needed to look as much like a work of art as what hung on the Amadeo walls. No thoughtful gifts, no family heirlooms. Nothing of value—financial, sentimental, or existential. A box full of empty tchotchkes.

People rich in one thing are rich in everything. Who knew love could actually protect you? A gift or inheritance could be what keeps the blood in your body rather than spilled in a Nashville alley.

Lisa scrolls the Facebook group, searching for mentions of stores outside the South Side still stocked with silver, starts typing a comment, then deletes it. Better not elicit suggestions before she's ready to drive to wherever this treasure is buried. Her cache will be long gone before she takes Koko back upstairs and changes into something more presentable than flannel pajama pants and a baggy Yuengling T-shirt acquired during some promo at Jake's. No one will take her seriously as a buyer. Any transactions at the values listed today will max out her credit cards, but no shopkeeper needs to know that.

She's been following Koko's lead, eyes and mind focused on her phone and her new quest for silver, and finally reenters the physical realm to realize they're crossing the alley, away from the warehouse.

"C'mon, Koko." Lisa pulls the leash. "It's time to head back. I know you don't know what's going on, but I've gotta find the supplies that'll protect us, and I can't be walking around all day with you to find the worst smells in the South Side."

Koko pulls against the leash.

"Jeez, girl, what is that? You don't want to get closer to something that smells like—oh shit."

In Lisa's senior year of college, her Drawing 4 professor, Mr. Gak, was notoriously hard to please. Lisa had dreaded his class since hearing rumblings her freshman year: A students receiving C's, C students failing. Sure, art is subjective—some will always see the avant-garde as degenerate—to some degree, but there is a delineation between good and bad. That's what they were in school to learn, right?

Mr. Gak seemed to think everything that came through his classroom was bad. And, after he was done figuratively ripping apart a drawing—more painful than the story of literal destruction with no judgment on quality imparted by the earlier, nicer teacher—he often referenced a former student.

The era was never mentioned; she could have been in his class decades ago, based on Mr. Gak's age and unspecified story setting. All the upbraided current students knew was that once upon a time, there was a girl who drew dead birds for an entire semester. And she was brilliant.

Always missing from the recounting was how this student found so many dead birds to sketch. Even in an urban area, pigeons don't just fly into telephone wires and behead themselves with the frequency to enable a four-month study of their carcasses. Some students checked the microfiche in the school library to find out if any former art students were jailed for serial murder and became the John Wayne Gacy of the women's prison.

And where was the challenge in sketching death anyway? Wasn't the skill in imparting a personality to a static rendering? Isn't that the brilliance of the *Mona Lisa*? The glint in her eyes, the enigmatic smile denoting the character and temper of this woman centuries after her death? Keeping long-gone subjects alive for eternity as they were in life, not in some vampiric sublife; isn't that at least part of what art is about?

There is nothing Lisa wants to immortalize in the scene in front of her. Not the blood spattered on the wooden palette in the weeds leaning against the old, stained retaining wall. Not the matted gray fur, sticking out at odd angles, the dried blood acting as pomade. And certainly not the gash on the neck that nearly severed the raccoon's head and left it at the angle of Klimt's *Eve*.

She doesn't want to remember it, much less paint it. She wants to scream, but she swallows it. There's no imminent danger. It's the thought of another pulsing paw added to the suspicious animal deaths map displayed on the national morning news. This one right on top of an arrow marking, YOU ARE HERE.

She does not want to be HERE at the scene of a crime perpetrated by some fiend that wasn't quite ready to give a human a back-alley tracheostomy, easing into blood drinking with rabid trash eaters. One of them would have to get out of there. And one of them was dead.

Lawrenceville is what South Side should have been. The historic buildings lining the main drag are practically as indistinguishable as early Braque and Picasso to the casual observer. The difference is that more of the buildings on Lawrenceville's Butler Street are occupied. And the denizens keep oyster bars, shoe stores, a French bakery, plant shops, and a pawnshop Lisa has ventured across the river to find in business.

It's not her first choice. Like most people walking through its doors, a pawnshop is the last resort. A hospice for strangers' treasures. Her first choices—any of the six piercers in South Side—had all sold out of silver jewelry in the hour between when they opened and when Lisa awoke. Apparently, she slept through lines forming outside every jewelry store in Pittsburgh. This was worse than what she heard about getting into the Louvre.

In her hours of news consumption while fashioning crosses, she'd heard little about silver. That must have been on a different channel.

At least the pawnshop has no line outside. By the look of it as she swings open the creaky door, no customers either. Maybe someone so resourceful as to make a lethal stake out of a canvas stretcher thinks differently from the fools who stand in line.

Glass cases—which may actually be plastic of the bulletproof variety—form a U-shape from knee to chest. About enough space for two Lisas or one portly shopkeeper from behind the counter to the wall and its collection of guitars, framed posters, and weapons. It's like the prize counter at the arcade: not the neon nostalgia created by Hollywood, but the grungy, grimy, gritty reality in shades of brown, olive, and gray. And these were no treasures, just a good deal due to a stranger's bad luck.

"Sold my last silver 10 minutes ago," the man behind the counter says.

If Lisa were a vampire, she'd be compelled to count the greasy hairs combed over his glistening bald pate. It wouldn't take her long.

The shop isn't like the ones on TV where precious items are displayed with care and cleanliness to clarify their value for people like Lisa, who now thinks maybe she shouldn't have gone for quantity over quality in her jewelry.

"You sure you don't have any left? I don't need jewelry. I'd take cutlery or—"

"Lady, if I had it, I'd sell it. Days like this don't come around often. Got more sales before noon than I sometimes do in a month. I tell ya, some weird folk gonna wind up rich off this whole vampiric panic."

"Rich isn't going to mean anything if you can't protect yourself."

THEY DRINK OUR BLOOD

"Well, if that's what you're worried about, I got you covered. I can't sell you a gun, but see this sword on the wall?" Lisa nods at the shiny blade as long as one of her legs. If only it was made of silver. But through her research at red lights on the drive over, she knows silver is way too malleable to make a traditional weapon. "May not be silver, but a Claymore's enough to cut off a vampire's head."

"I'm not really looking to chop off a head. More like ward them off."

"No one leaves the house looking to decapitate some undead teenager. But sometimes you got no choice but to stand your ground. If you can't fend' em off, chop 'em off. That's what I always say."

Lisa scans the shelves, but nothing catches her eye.

"See, mister, I'm an artist, and I can be real creative with anything you have to give me. Even the tiniest bit of silver can help. I went to art school. My medium is oil paint, but I took sculpture and worked with metals some and—"

"I'm sorry, lady, but I've got nothing for you. I suggest you get yourself a weapon. Silver's not a stake."

"I already got a stake." Lisa turns from the corpulent pawnbroker behind his grimy case of baseball cards and gold class rings. She steps toward the door, back to the now overcast afternoon with such cloud cover it seems even the heavens are conspiring with the vampires to block out the sun.

"Hey, lady, I just thought of something. I think I can help you out."

She follows him around a dusty, decorative suit of armor, which can't possibly have more monetary than sentimental value.

"Kicking myself for not thinking of this earlier, but truth is with the rush this morning, I didn't get much time to think." He speaks, but his mind is on the task of prying open an iPhone with a small, flat-head screwdriver.

"There's not a lot of silver in here. I don't know how much good it'll do you. Depends on how bad you need it. And dunno what an artist can do with a logic board."

He pushes metal parts and plastic parts out of the way with his screwdriver, mumbling about it being a good thing he's not going to have to reassemble this baby until, "Aha! Here you go." He hands the tiny rectangle to Lisa.

"I'll figure something out. Can I get another one?"

"OK, lady, but I gotta be honest and charge you for two whole phones. These are just shells now, and I can't very well put 'em back on the shelves and sell 'em to folks'll wanna be making calls."

Fifteen minutes later, Lisa places her two tiny rectangles in the center console of her car. Some people may be getting rich off the vampires, but Lisa isn't one of them.

Can a vampire survive in daylight when most of the sun is hidden behind clouds? Probably not. And besides, that's what the $460 of silver in the cupholder was for—a vaccine against attacks.

She logs on to the ride-share app. Pickup at Allegheny Cemetery? Oh, thank God. It's the bar across the street from the main entrance. She accepts.

Taylor looks to be in her late 20s, dressed smart casual, maybe leaving early from an office happy hour. At 3 p.m. on a Monday? Leaving late from a liquid lunch meeting? Some hip startup using phrases like "work-life balance" and "flexible hours" that people say is code for "work is life" and "more hours"?

"Good on you for supporting your local bars during this time," Lisa says as Taylor gets into the car. "I know how bad they're hurting with no one wanting to be out at night and all that. Some folks are gonna get rich off all this, but it sure won't be the bar owners."

"Actually, I'm their account manager at the ad agency I work for, so I wasn't supporting them as a customer."

"Then you know how tough it is for bars right now. I seen on the news some bars are voluntarily closing to try to keep people from going out at night. Keep them home and safe, you know? And that may be all well and good if you've got the money to just close your doors and your staff doesn't mind being furloughed and what not."

Nineteen minutes later, Taylor becomes Eugene riding from upscale Shadyside to the airport. The highway isn't wide enough to handle rush hour. From frequent peeks in the rear-view mirror, Lisa gauges him her contemporary, albeit having taken the road more frequently traveled. Much of his life spent literally and figuratively in bumper-to-bumper traffic, but still allowing time for a shave, a tailoring, and a trip to the gym.

Eugene's headed to the airport, then to Las Vegas. No, he's not taking some weird, wild trip to live it up on a Monday; Vegas is home. And, no, he wasn't living it up in Pittsburgh either. He was here for a conference, got stuck through the weekend for a Monday morning meeting. Sure, he went out at night downtown after the exhibition hall closed for the evening, had some of the best brick-oven pizza of his life. "Overall, the food downtown was just as good as any on the vaunted Strip. Better dollar for dollar."

Was he worried about being out at night, on foot, in a strange city?

"Worried? At night? I've lived in Vegas for 16 years. Your art galleries and theaters downtown didn't worry me. No one else seemed to be worried either." He catches her eyes in the rearview mirror. "We're all out-of-towners; what don't we know?"

Lisa thinks, releases her foot from the brake for about three seconds before depressing it again. Theaters, art galleries. What would teenagers, regardless of their era, want with the ballet? The opera? The Pittsburgh Symphony Orchestra? Snooze-fests to them. Places where their grandparents would hang. No, no kids. So no vampires.

"I don't spend a lot of time downtown. I know there's all the galleries and I been meaning to check them out, but it just keeps getting away from me. There was an exhibit just last spring—an installation with LEDs, about the interplay between light and shadow that we fail to notice as we move about in the world. The artist and I went to school together, but I missed it. Every time I thought about going, I had a better reason to stay home. That's about when I started to wonder what I was doing with my life, how I wasn't contributing much and I just couldn't care about the interplay between light and shadow and couldn't believe Lynne—that's the artist—did either. Seemed to me she'd just made that up to pretend there was some meaning behind her pretty light projections. Like she was fooling herself to think what she was doing mattered to others and not just because she didn't want to get a job as a nurse or something, you know?"

"I live in Vegas. We don't pretend anything has meaning. Our whole city is just an elaborate escape where we can pretend to experience the world." Eugene stares out the window at the quaint billboards advertising local plumbing businesses.

"I've been thinking that's a lot of what art is, too. Bring our emotions so you can experience them without any real-world consequences."

"No risk, all reward." His cliché is almost dismissive as he keeps gazing at the office buildings off the side of the road.

"Tell that to any of the artists Stalin sent to the Gulag." Eugene finally refocuses ahead, reinvesting in the conversation.

"They took risks, but it was about expressing themselves, wasn't it? It was still all about them."

"No way," Eugene says. "Those artists were fighting for something in a way that's so much more enduring than the the Soviets' mass slaughter. Great art captures a universal feeling. It may not be curing cancer, but how many people has an artist saved by just providing evidence that there was someone else out there who felt the same thing?"

"Even if it's not what the artist meant?"

"Who cares what the artist meant? I mean, practically speaking, if it resonates with you, pulls you in, isn't art doing its job? Didn't you have something that you felt was speaking directly to you?"

She did. And the accompanying Stendhal syndrome that sent her on the beaten path she'd been traveling until about six months ago.

The app dings, and she's reminded to exit the highway at the airport. Those last few miles of the journey finally experienced at or above the speed limit become a blur in her thoughts. What were these past 30 years for? Would she feel complete, realized, if she'd had the career of Jeff Koons?

If Eugene doesn't tap the trunk, Lisa will pull away from the Southwest gate with his bag. She ends the ride, and another request flashes on the screen. Kaden in a suburb on the way back home from the airport needs a lift to an address mere blocks away from home. She accepts that last fare of the day.

Lisa has never been able to articulate the feeling art brings her. It's not intellectual. If it were, she wouldn't have to read the descriptions of the pieces on the gallery walls, look back at the piece, and try to connect the words with the image. It's more than emotional; it's a chemical reaction, an endorphin surge followed by a sense of peace. Euphoria. It hits her pleasure centers as she loses herself in a Joan Miró painting.

Lost time.

Lost in her own creations. Hours spent alone in a semiconscious state, letting the deepest, weirdest recesses of her subconscious flow onto the canvas in such abstraction their meaning is obscured to Lisa and any viewer.

And that's the inkling that's been in the back of her conscious mind these past several months since Amadeo's closed: Her pursuit of art has been less about creation and more about escape, hiding in plain sight, creating opaque images, cowardly claiming their meaning was in the viewer's interpretation.

Building a wall around herself, using self-expression to hide who she was while still seeking recognition. Is she truly as empty, as devoid of meaning as her squares? Is that all she has to give? A meaningless contribution from a meaningless life.

Unless this recent foray into the banal mechanisms that keep modern society running is her purpose. She takes people where they need to go.

"Arriving to pick up Kaden," the app announces as Lisa pulls up to a red-brick suburban two-story, its address illuminated above the door. Illuminated because sometime in Lisa's reverie, the sky turned from gray to black.

And there's no time to open the door, unbuckle, pop the trunk, and dig for the tire-changing supplies in her trunk that could serve as weapons for the desperate before the hooded figure reaches the Chevy HHR.

The figure is lanky with long legs striding up the path that bisects the lawn. The darkness simplifies the form of the young man into little more than a shadow.

Lisa grabs the logic boards from the cupholder, looks around the immaculate car. Nothing to make a necklace, as there would have been during her former career. Without glue, she can't even wear them on the USB cable.

The figure approaches. He's close enough that the dark hoodie is now revealed as blue, with the emblem of Lisa's alma mater on the chest. She shoves the logic boards into the elastic tie-dye band covering most of her scruffy, matted hair. One at each temple, exposed enough that no vampire could miss when leaning into her neck.

The back driver's-side door opens. Either a text saying, "Your driver, Lisa, is here in a gray HHR," is an invitation to enter or Kaden is just a teenager.

He slides into the back seat.

"Kaden?"

"Hey." Indifferent, like a teenager. Isn't part of a vampire's allure that he seems to give you his undivided attention, makes you feel like no one else exists? Not dismissive and uninterested in anyone over 20. Lisa's heart rate slows. She exhales. Vampires are supposed to have charisma. Kaden does not.

"South Side?"

No response.

Lisa twists her body, grabs the console so she can swivel and see into the back seat. Sort of. She's never understood the lack of dome lighting in the HHR. Next car she'll test drive at night. Even in the dark, her movement is enough to get his attention. From the blue hood pulled tight around his chin, his eyes meet hers.

"South Side?"

"Yeah."

"South Side's a good part of town. Lotta good folks live down there. All sorts of folks of all ages have called it home for decades. It gets a bad rap for being a 24/7 party town, but it's mostly residential. What brings you there on a Monday night?"

Silence. No, not exactly. Pulsing, rhythmic, tinny static. He's listening to music, his ear buds hidden under his hood. Lisa focuses on the road ahead, the suburbs where so many of the people she's encountered have disappeared from her life. Comfort. Safety. They don't have vampires in the suburbs. Yes! She needs to stop worrying; it's just another brooding teen in the back seat.

She turns right onto Amsterdam Street per the app's instructions and slams the gas pedal to give the HHR a chance to climb the steep hill in second gear. The rpm hits the same as her heart rate did when she saw she was picking up a teenager after dark. Glancing at the rearview, she notices a parade of headlights, all slowed by her laborious ascent. White, glowing bocce balls behind her.

But no Kaden.

The outline of the blue hood with no face inside.

Could it be a trick of the light or, in this case, a trick of the darkness, of the sparse light poles and the HHR's absurdly small windows? She can't gaze back into the mirror to search for his face without careening into whatever awaits in the black beyond the sidewalks. Yet every fleeting glance reveals the blue of the hood with no Kaden inside.

Maybe it was like how the camera screen—in her year-long stint as a school photographer in those low times between college and the gallery when she was desperate for work in something, anything she could call artistic—lost the darker-skinned children in the black backdrop. Maybe the rearview mirror had the same effect that caused half the city school yearbook photos to be conspicuously off-center.

Maybe Lisa had just never noticed because it had never occurred to her that her passengers would not have reflections. Now she's on alert, and she silently castigates herself for not checking as soon as the silent, gaunt figure stooped to crawl into the back seat. She hasn't been so scared in a car since a joyride with Berty back in college when he was behind the wheel. This time, she is in control. It's her hands on the wheel.

The car crests the latest hill and Lisa lets it roll, picking up speed, leaving the soft, white orbs behind until the back window is as empty as an orange square on canvas.

The speedometer on the app turns red, flashes. The machine still thinks speed is the greatest risk to safety. It keeps flashing red until she slows at the light to turn right on the four-lane thoroughfare. Lisa relaxes her death grip on the wheel. The last of several rush hours is still filling both lanes on each side of the median. It's a landscape of splotchy dots on black, an inverted Damien Hirst.

The street has enough cars where someone would notice if the thing calling itself Kaden were to suddenly lurch over the driver's seat and sink its fangs into Lisa's neck. She would surely lose all bodily control. Her hands would abandon the wheel in some lizard-brain instinct, detecting the greater danger to her person than the multistep process that starts with freewheeling and ends with ribs shattered by an airbag. We didn't evolve to control tons of heavy machinery. Her feet would be next, slamming into the floor to give her stability (in theory) as she wrestled the immortal fiend from her neck.

They would wind up in one of three places. If both feet landed on the floor, she'd careen into 45 mph traffic. If one foot hit the accelerator, the same thing would happen—only faster. If one foot suddenly depressed the brake, the car behind her would collide with her rear bumper and send her to the same place. In any scenario she can conjure, the HHR would be jackknifed into rush hour traffic and nothing would prevent her from being anything less than a curiosity for the rubberneckers and a recipient of window-side vitriol from the motorists who can't emotionally handle another stoppage after they've finally made it through the tunnel.

This thought, such as it is, brings comfort.

Turning right, she joins the procession. It's almost funereal, mourning the loss of freedom. In her 23 years since college, as what pollsters would consider technically a member of the workforce, Lisa has never waited in line to get to work. Bathrooms at bars, entries at gallery openings, checkout counters at art supply stores behind the housewives and their carts loaded with fake flowers and no price tags, but never to arrive at work. Maybe there was something noble, philosophical, existential about her commitment to freedom and her passion. Or maybe it was just another selfish urge not to spend two hours a day doing something she didn't want to do.

The GPS knows nothing good comes from sitting in traffic and directs her away from the Liberty Tunnel and through the main drag of one of the hilltop neighborhoods with enough pedestrians that Lisa no longer feels her heart in her throat. The GPS gets greedy, tries to save her 15 seconds by directing her to the narrow, dark roads that twist into an Escher drawing down the mountain to the South Side. She doesn't need the GPS anymore anyway. She knows where she's taking Kaden. It's mere blocks from her home.

She pulls onto the wide, cratered road in a part of the neighborhood between the residences and the river, forgotten by everyone but one developer who recently proposed building a housing complex. Lisa had opposed the plan on principle, but maybe the lights and people that would come with a modern building would be worth the collective rent hikes.

An apartment complex nestled between an old factory and the train tracks may be hard to rent, but it surely would necessitate bulldozing the building where she stops the car.

Kaden utters a gruff thanks and exits. His head bowed, typing into his phone, he saunters to the former administrative office of the long-gone Nova Metals Company. Nearly hidden by weeds, the one-story structure looks like it's already seen the apocalypse.

As much as we try with our asphalt and herbicides, we're still losing the war against nature.

Kaden reaches the door. It's his last test. If he opens it and walks in, Lisa can breathe easy.

He knocks.

THEY DRINK OUR BLOOD

He waits.

The door opens.

He enters.

However little her squares—and sometimes trapezoids—contributed to society, as an artist, she never thought she was supporting degeneration. How much damage can an ignored artist do whose works are primarily displayed on the backsides of newer identical works?

Nothing like a cog in this banal machine.

Lisa takes vampires where they need to go.

She assuages her guilt the next morning by delivering vampire-repelling crosses where they need to go.

Number 59 goes to Carlos for his stained-glass studio on the third floor. He already wears a tasteful gold cross around his neck, thanks Lisa profusely, and hangs the canvas cross on the inside of the door with its creator as a witness. Fifty-eight and 57 are two of Lisa's favorites, so she presents them to fellow oil painter Margot and muralist Nicolette to make the best possible first impression on her neighbors of the past three months. Fifty-six she stashes in the elevator for communal emergency use. Fifty-five now hangs below the signed 8x10 of Tom Savini posing with a monster head at the Bat Cave.

After talking to the man who introduces himself as Zack the bar owner, Lisa feels particularly proud of her mission.

"I can tell you we never would have hung a cross in this bar, but that's a work of art. Something about the way it changes from black to orange in the center, almost like a reverse black hole. Like, I don't know why, but it feels like hope," the owner says.

Lisa thinks back to Sonia's argument about art saving lives and wonders if Zack would have felt the same about the shapes and colors and gradients if its form did not have the function of fending off a bloodsucking fiend.

Fifty-four is at a pizza shop, 53 a piercing joint still sold out of silver. Fifty-two through 49 she hands to various acquaintances she recognizes from decades in the neighborhood—by face, not name. Forty-eight, 46, 34, and 31 are at tattoo shops; 47, 44, 36, 32, and 30 at barber shops; 45 at a dog groomer; 43, 42, 41, 40, 39, 38, 37, 36, 33, 29, and 28 in an array of establishments that peddle vape cartridges and dubiously legal marijuana derivatives. Lisa has 27 in hand when she arrives at the salon.

"Lisa! Did I miss your name on the schedule?" Ophelia, her beach waves sharing a design with Sonia's makeshift room dividers, hops up from a styling chair in the otherwise empty salon.

"No. I just came by to deliver you something I hope you won't need."

"Well, I hope you're delivering you because I need clients." She waves her arm as if to present—ta-da!—a magical customer-appearing trick. "And what you need is a style sesh. Geez, Lisa, your hair was so hip for the gallery last time I saw you. Now you're hiding under that ratty bandana. What happened?"

"The gallery closed."

"What? When?"

"Like six months ago. So, I don't really need a hip haircut anymore, y'know. No one cares much what their ride-share driver looks like, and seeing how funds are tight, I didn't think I could justify a styling if it wasn't all that necessary anymore. It's not like a driver has to look a certain way. So, you know, I've been more focused on doing my part to help make the world go round instead of fussing about myself."

"That's great, but you can't forget about self-love. If you're not caring for yourself, how can you expect to give the best care to the world?" She raises her threaded eyebrows. "Sit down. Let's get that hair cleaned up."

Lisa finds herself in the chair, unaware of having walked to it, setting her Ikea bag filled with vampire repellent on the floor. In the mirror, even under the forgiving lights of the salon meant to make you leave thrilled with the results and blaming yourself for never looking as good as you did when you left your appointment, a cabbie stares at the onetime artist. Her pale cheeks are a farmland topography as seen from an airplane—creases and puffs she doesn't recall seeing last time she sat here.

"The news said all the women drained to death by vampires had dark hair."

"Perfect! We'll bleach these roots after we chop a few inches off." Ophelia drapes the black cloth over Lisa, snapping it tight against the thin skin of her neck. It's constricting, but nothing compared to a sharp canine in her jugular, so Lisa doesn't mention it. Ophelia's acrylic nails, precision-painted with spiderwebs— a level of artistic detail for which Lisa never had the patience—pry the bandana off, revealing the early stages of a dreadlock.

"Those are interesting earrings," Ophelia says.

"They're circuit boards. I know they're not all that fashionable yet, but if the silver shortage continues, you're gonna see a lot more people wearing them for protection."

"Silver shortage? What kind of silver?" Ophelia tugs a comb through Lisa's accidental hair knitting.

"Any silver." Lisa winces as gray strands dislodge from her scalp. "Purer the better, as that'll burn vampires, not just deter them. I think—"

"Sterling silver?"

"Maybe. I tried to find sterling silver yesterday as it'd be in bigger chunks than I've got here on these boards. I guess they're OK for now, though. I had a close encounter last night, and I think these saved me, small as they are, and how the silver is, you know—"

"I have loads of sterling silver. My grandparents used to take me out West like every summer. Hopi and Navajo jewelry. You're saying people are going nuts for it?"

"It repels vampires. It's sold out everywhere."

"Hmm. So, I could probably make a killing on Facebook Marketplace right now."

"Yeah, maybe, but you gotta keep some for yourself since you live around here and South Side is like ground zero in Pittsburgh. You gotta protect yourself getting home late after work. That's actually why I came down here, to give you something else to make sure you'd be safe if any of the vamp—"

"Let's go over to the sink."

"If any of the vampires get invited in by accident, you'll have a cross on the wall they won't like much. It'll help you identify the vampires from the regular teenagers since it's kinda hard to tell and all."

Lisa reclines in the seat, and cool water rushes over her hair. Ophelia's fingers massage her scalp. So soothing, the occasional scraping of acrylic nails doesn't disturb her sudden tranquility, more relaxed than her sleep since the news from Nashville broke. She deserves this treat after such hard work. And it's as altruistic as it is pleasurable. With the news reports of chronic neighborhood malfeasance, all types of businesses are suffering. Yes, this haircut is her civic duty just as much as distributing crosses or alerting the Down Low group about mutilated raccoon carcasses.

And anyway, the new look (or the old look made new again) will help her mission. Business owners will be more receptive to decorative crosses when delivered by someone who looks like an artist. And maybe, when her impasto crosses have deterred more vampires from bars than the most mountainous bouncers, when skeptical barflies like that Hank down at the Bat Cave shove one in a fanged face about to bite, starving the fiend from its sustenance so it stumbles in a ravenous, weakened daze into the street to be crushed by a semi and turning the creature's rib into an internal stake—maybe after seeing her art do some actual good, maybe then she'd at last be a real artist.

Neighbors may even pay for the crosses as functional art. Maybe society will never be in the throes of a vampire epidemic again. Maybe it will become endemic, and we'll be in a state of constant vigilance. Maybe the nation will reach a point when circuit board earrings and pocket stakes are comedy fodder. We'll laugh at the paranoia but keep an oil-painted cross on the wall just to be safe. Get lost in the thick paint, the layers of color on color, discover new depths in the simple composition every time we glance above the mantel.

The flashing red and blue lights in the mirror save her from the fate of Narcissus.

"Hey!" Ophelia stops cutting. "Hold still, or it's gonna be messy uneven, not artsy uneven."

"Something happened out there. Maybe someone was attacked who could have used one of my crosses . . . "

"Something is always happening here. Stalkers. Weirdos. Shady real estate deals. Hit-and-runs."

The storefront windows barely muffle the sirens. Flashing lights multiply in the mirror.

"Lisa, sit down, c'mon. I got one more section to highlight."

Having slipped from the chair, Lisa scampers to the front window. A squad car, jackknifed across 18th Street, blocks entry onto Carson from the end that crosses train tracks and eventually ends at the river. Three other cruisers parked near the intersection contribute to the light show.

"Something bad happened."

"And the sooner you come back to this chair, the sooner you can go see what's going on."

THEY DRINK OUR BLOOD

It seems a waste to walk back to the chair for a single highlight, but she understands the frustration of leaving a work unfinished. As soon as the foil is wrapped around the final chunk of hair, six inches shorter than when she walked into the salon, Lisa exits into the darkness of 6 p.m. post-daylight saving time. Maybe vampires will conflate the Medusa-like snakes of aluminum shooting off her head with silver. Maybe they'll see her salon cloak and assume she's one of them. She squeezes the stake concealed under the black nylon shift just in case.

Ophelia said she had 30 minutes before her hair would start to fry like a vampire in the sun. That was certainly enough time to reach the WTF News van parked halfway to 19th Street.

A reporter, hair as blonde as Lisa's would be in half an hour, speaks into a WTF News microphone from the center of the wide sidewalk where wild vampires marauded to kick off the weekend terror. Lisa steps closer to the van, staying in the shadows in her black cloak, street and police car lights reflecting off her metal dreads, close enough to hear the breaking news.

"That's right. We're reporting on a vampire murder on the South Side where a woman, covered in blood, flagged down a patrolling officer to report her boyfriend was attacked and his blood drained from his neck by a gang of roving vampires. While we don't yet know the details, we understand the victim was in his tent on the river trail when at least seven youths tore through the fabric and attacked. The witness, whose identity is currently being withheld by police, fled up 18th to Carson Street. Police and the coroner's office are at the crime scene, and the witness has been transported to an area hospital for evaluation."

When Lisa's hair is foil free, dry, and too blonde to fit the pattern of recent vampire attack victims and her bag of 26 crosses is back on her table for continued distribution the next day and Koko is walked and fed, the official WTF News report has softened to "a deadly attack with possible vampiric motives."

THEY DRINK OUR BLOOD

In the morning, after a long, deep sleep—finally, after nights up too late becoming part of the solution—the Facebook group has a different take on the murder.

Dorian Black: Yinz see this shit?

Lisa doesn't read the linked article, just the headline: "Man dead in South Side, girlfriend claims vampire attack."

Molly Denson: This is getting crazy.

Dev Martel: Why are we such a vampire hot bed all of a sudden?

Cody Adway: Because we don't get sun here.

Joe Lindo: This story is bullshit. My tent was next to theirs over the summer. Couple of tweakers, always fighting. That rip in the tent is from July when they had a fight over which one of them lost their stash or some shit. No way that junkie bitch didn't kill him and try to blame vampires.

Ken Smith: Damn, dude. Judge much?

Joe Lindo: Why would a vampire want junkie blood? Wouldn't they smell it was rotten or some shit?

Lisa scrolls to the next post. Vampire or not, a man was murdered down the street.

Mimi Castenovich: Another thing to watch for.

The link opens a TikTok video. Lisa clicks. The window fills with a bad green screen, about as technologically advanced as the ones at early '90s amusement parks in front of which she and her junior high friends would lip sync. It takes 30 years to bring technology from a paid service to a free app that, instead of projecting psychedelic patterns, lets you talk over a still photo of a chubby, baby-faced Latino in a sweater vest.

The text on screen says, "4 things to know about familiars." Lisa increases the volume on her phone, hearing the woman with the cat-eye glasses and tiger-striped hair speak into a microphone so small it appears the woman and the device are in two different perspectives.

"Although they want to be, familiars are not vampires. They are humans, no special powers, just like you and me. Yes, they may eat live insects, but that's just a way to try to emulate the bloodlust of the vampire. They do not derive special powers from drinking rodent blood or sucking down worms.

"Two. They keep odd hours. No, they are not nocturnal. You will still see them during the day because that is the time they need to take care of vampire business. Think banking, visiting the post office, getting capes dry-cleaned. These are things a vampire cannot do because of the hours. A familiar is like a personal assistant. You'll see a familiar busy during the day with these tasks, but their evenings will be mysteriously full with other business."

The background changes to Tom Waits in a 19th-century asylum.

"Three. A familiar's main role is to procure victims for the vampire.

"Four. Familiars keep vampires safe. You may be thinking that's crazy. Vampires are these immortal beings with superhuman strength who can mesmerize our weak human minds, seduce us with their sparkles, and dig their razor-sharp teeth into our necks to drain us of our life. They are the top of the food chain. They have no predators. What do they need protection from?

"Well, sunlight, for one. Someone needs to make sure the drapes are drawn. We already talked about handling administrative duties. That keeps them incognito. Though they're powerful, they have to remain secret because humans, though far less genetically gifted with less cunning, less strength, duller incisors, inability to transmogrify, are a danger to vampires in large enough groups with the right weapons. So a familiar may go stake, pun intended, out a location as a potential hunting ground where there are no Van Helsings out there to ambush them."

The video ends abruptly, then starts to replay. Lisa closes the window and resumes scrolling the feed in the South Side Down Low Facebook group.

Mike Carloni: C'mon down to Jake's Mistake for happy hours 1 pm to sunset! We've got the most vampire-proof bar in South Side. $4 well drinks, $3 drafts, and a free garlic clove! Hang with us and get home before dark.

Lisa decides to do just that.

The cardboard—probably the interior of a beer bottle box by the look of the crease at the center—duct-taped to the door of Jake's Mistake reads, "Vampires NOT welcome" in a black Sharpie scrawl. With her 26 crosses in the Ikea bag slung over her shoulder, Lisa turns the knob and enters. Inside, the overwhelming smell of ashtrays, smoke, and garlic is barely more welcoming to the living. Maybe that's why she's the first "happy hours" customer.

"Nice sign." She takes a seat at the bar, not so close to the entrance as to be the first line of defense if the sign fails and not so far as to be in a similar position if vampires invade through the back door of the unused kitchen.

"Used to hang one that said 'No Fat Chicks' back in the Delta Kap days," Mike says, Miller High Life bottle in hand, from the stool he's pulled behind the bar.

"Real nice," Jodi says, rolling her eyes and sliding a Straub draft to Lisa without asking.

"Hey! Not saying I'd do that now. As long as you wanna drink my beer, not my blood, everyone's welcome here."

Out of habit and to avoid Mike's confirmation-seeking gaze, Lisa looks up at the TV and its black screen. "No news today?"

"Hell no! Nothing shuts down a party like that depressing shit. We gotta give this place some life again."

"I told you before, Mike, most folks still gotta work early afternoons," Jodi says.

"They're all collecting unemployment. That's why I can barely keep this place staffed. Or they're . . . " He raises his hands to air quote, the beer dangling from his fingers, "working from home."

As he closes the quote, the Miller High Life bottle slips. It's early enough that he hasn't had enough to dull his reflexes, just the levee that prevents everything from his brain flooding out of his mouth, and he catches it as foam sloshes on his cargo pants. Agitated, more foam rises from the lip and spills over the mouth. Before it reaches his hand, Mike chugs down the beer, sucking up the lather. Lisa sips hers. The aftertaste is lotion, coating her mouth like it, too. She runs her fingers down the outside of the glass, painting lines in the condensation, doing something, anything, because of the obligation you feel to entertain when you know you're being watched.

"Your hair is different," Mike says.

"It's actually the way it used to be." Lisa stares at her condensation art.

"Hah!" If the bar was full, conversations would have stopped to discover the reason for the deafening guffaw. "You gals can certainly make time stop, can't you? I do that, my bros never stop ragging I got asshole hairs on my head." He rubs the inch-long brown hairs struggling to cover his scalp, making a valiant last stand against the shiny baldness encroaching from his temples. "You look like one of those Japanese cartoons."

"Like manga?"

"I don't know what the fuck it's called, but it's got the big eyes and wacky hair."

"Thanks."

"It's not a bad thing."

"Thanks." To occupy her hands, Lisa lifts the beer to her mouth, takes a sip. The low late-'90s alternative is the only sound in the dark space, all the light that enters obscured through Coke bottle windows. It feels like her senses are dulled. Lisa puts the beer down, almost reaches for it again to fill an empty moment, to pass the time. Instead, she reaches for her phone.

"You see my post about happy hour?" Mike tosses his empty bottle in the trash can, reaches under the bar for another.

"Yeah, that's how I knew to come down."

Lisa scrolls her feed, sees the post again. Still no comments. She considers giving it a like, decides against it as that will notify Mike, and, after all these nights in the bar, may finally let him remember her name.

"Safest place in South Side right here." Mike rises from the stool, his throne from which he rules his meager domain. "See all that garlic?" He spreads his arms, gesturing to nowhere in particular. He doesn't need to. It's everywhere. Mesh sleeves filled with the pungent allium hang from light fixtures. Bulbs are glued to the walls. Little jars of minced garlic in olive oil sit in the center of the high-tops like votive candles.

"It's hard to miss."

"He hit all the grocery stores before they put the limits on," Jodi says.

"Damn right. After that meeting at the church. After everyone laughed at you when you said we gotta prepare for vampires—"

"Not everyone laughed at me."

"They all laughed, but the joke's gonna be on them ' cause I went and cleared out all the garlic—fresh, jarred, bottled, all of it."

"What you see here isn't all of it," Jodi says. "I made some runs of my own. We're stocked in the back. We weren't kidding when we said we've got bulbs to give away. Support everyone supporting us."

"Everyone else getting rationed, and we're fucking rich. And that's not all." Mike leans under the bar, pulls out a case of Miller High Life, and reaches behind it.

When Lisa sees the axe, her first thought is, "Here's Johnny!" and her teenage attempt to enjoy the horror her classmates seemed to love. Though Mike's voice is raised a level too loud for the bar, his grip on the axe is firm. Is that better or worse than the weapon slipping from his drunken hands?

"In case any get in here."

"Some old head thinking he's being a gentleman holding the door open for a sexy young vamp," Jodi adds.

"We see one of them fiends going for a neck, I swing this into its neck before it's got the time to bite."

"I read it takes a stake to the heart or cutting off a head," Lisa says, her nervous fingers stroking her own weapon concealed in her shoulder bag.

"Oh, this'll cut off a head."

"It will." Jodi nods. "It's as sharp as one of those guillo-things. And this'll stab through the ribs better than any stake." She pulls a switchblade from her pocket.

Lisa's lessons in anatomy delved only so deep as to explain how the interior affected the exterior. What everything under the surface did was less important than how to depict it. Is either the blade or the stake capable of piercing the heart? The stake is a last resort, of course. As Lisa's sure the blade and the axe are as well, if one of those things manages to get past the door and its forbidding sign, the garlic, and the crosses in her Ikea bag.

Jodi's knife is back in her pocket, but Mike cradles the axe, the red lights of the Bud Light sign glinting off the blade that is sharp enough to cut far deeper than any body parts covered in an Anatomy for Artists class and any supplies she's held on to from other college courses. To be anything close to lethal, you'd have to get creative in a way that challenges even a serial sketcher of dead birds.

The greatest danger Lisa encountered in her decades in art were table saws, which could inflict little more than superficial wounds on students hung over just enough to lose focus on tasks that require concentration. With their brain cells starved of nutrients not easily replenished by dining hall fare, the students smashed a thumb with a chisel, nicked a knuckle with a carving tool, took a splinter to the eye when whittling, and, worse case, lost a fingerprint to the saw.

Those students—the professors never knew their charges were impaired before or often even after an accident— didn't smell any worse than college art students usually did. They didn't slur their words, fall down, forget the alphabet. Their eyes weren't shrunk to glassy little beads that saw a different reality, a reality in which clocks melt and women are chests of drawers.

When that's what you see, you have no choice but to embark on an adventure. Take a swig from the malt liquor in the cupholder, and speed up on the one-way street, ramming other cars that deign to follow traffic laws. Lisa had forgotten most of that evening as a passenger in her friend Berty's car, but she remembered his eyes and made excuses to flee when she saw them transform anytime from that night on. His shiny, quick-blinking eyes were like windows into that other world. Not blue skies and cumulus clouds; it's more like a self-portrait with a severed ear.

The axe with its guillotine-sharp blade on his lap, Mike stares at Lisa with the same glassy eyes. What he's seeing and what messages are being transmitted to his addled brain, she doesn't know. She hoists the Ikea bag onto the bar.

"What's with the tarp?" Mike's interest lasts a second before the beads dart toward the creaking door and the glow of what passes for sunlight in Pittsburgh. He clutches the axe. Jodi smacks her hand over her hip pocket. The first thing Lisa sees is the bowler hat, then the Jake's Mistake crew relaxing.

"Sign outside says happy hour. You're all in here way too serious." Walter tosses his hat on the bar as he takes a seat near the entrance.

"Serious times, Walter." Jodi pours a generous double shot of Old Crow on the rocks and slides the glass to the regular.

"Why you got an axe?"

"You need a special kind of weapon to kill a vampire." Mike places the axe back under the bar. Lisa's heart slows down to the fat-burning zone.

"If your hands are lethal, you don't need a weapon."

"You can't cut off a head with your bare hands," Jodi says. "You can't even do that to a normal person, and they don't have immortality and whatever other special powers vampires do."

"You ever seen a vampire?" Walter asks.

THEY DRINK OUR BLOOD

"The way they're all over the place these days, I must've. But how do I know? That's what makes 'em so evil-like; they blend right in."

"You see them if you can't see them," Lisa says. Silence. Paradox requires explanation. "I picked up a ride the other night, this kid, and he was in the back seat. I could see him if I twisted around, but he didn't show in my rearview. No reflection. That's a mark of a vampire. I think it's because they don't have souls or something, but I saw it. I mean, I didn't see it. But that means I saw it, you know. My silver protected me, or else I'm sure I'd be like that woman in Nashville. And Annapolis. And the professor in Ithaca. And the dogs in Youngstown."

"The guttersnipe on the trail," Jodi says.

"I dunno. Last I saw on the news, they were saying vampires doubtful in that one."

"They're just saying that so we don't freak out. Get all this vampire news out then act like we're crazy for sharpening axes and buying up the garlic. They just want us so scared we keep watching updates, but they don't want us to defend ourselves." Mike ends his speech with a belch, eyes darting back and forth between his two customers until they settle on the Ikea bag.

Lisa pulls a cross from the bag and pushes it down the bar to Mike.

"Oh, sweet. We were gonna make some of these, weren't we, Jodi?"

"Mike tried with beer cases, but we couldn't get a straight line with the box cutter."

"And how's a piece of cardboard gonna scare off a vampire anyway? This is solid. And shit, you got a whole bag of them?"

"Yeah, I've been distributing them to all the businesses down here. Mount it on a wall, but in a place you can easily reach it just in case."

Mike pops off the stool, his beer bottle taking its turn to belch bubbles from its mouth where he abandons it on the counter to rummage through the Ikea bag.

"Fuck yeah! There's enough to cover the walls. Now we're really the safest bar on South Side." His mood—apparently as ephemeral as light on Monet's water lilies—lifted, the bar owner disappears into his unused kitchen.

"It's a nice gesture, but it won't protect you like knowing

martial arts," Walter says. "I seen beasts that'd make your head spin. Big, muscular hulking creatures with spikes in their necks and backs like a stegosaurus. Pointed tongues, bulging eyes. Creeping around, stealing souls and putting them in a basket. I snuck up—silent, not even a footstep—delivered a flying round kick right into his twisted spine, sent the monster down and the basket sailing through the air. But I caught it before any of the souls could escape." He nods his head, the way the sales trainer Camille hired instructed the staff to convince potential customers everything they were hearing was accurate and, yes, they really needed that abstract bust made of resin-coated mini-bagels and paper clips.

"You took down a soul-stealing bodybuilder with a single kick?" Jodi uses a tone usually reserved for a child, not a man 30 years her senior. It's not the reaction to a hero's story, but, then again, true heroes rarely volunteer to tell their tales.

"I'm a master of the art of hand-to-hand combat. You know that. It's why you need me around here."

"Which martial art?" Lisa asks. "My parents signed me up for tae kwon do in fourth grade, but I didn't stick with it because of all my art classes and—"

"I know tae kwon do, kung fu, muy thai, tae bo, pad thai, karate, jiujitsu, tai chi, kung pao. That's why these kids and these vampires don't worry me. I got' em all up in here." He points to his temple. "I'm vigilant. Learned from experience. Always be alert. Sometimes a little girl with a yellow flower wears a death mask."

"All right, so I don't have a lot of nails, but I got duct tape when they run out." Mike emerges from the kitchen.

"You're gonna nail your thumb to the wall you pick up another beer," Jodi says.

"Fuck that noise. I get these all up, and you all can drink without stressing. Safest place in South Side."

"You made these?" Walter asks in his thin voice, weakened from whiskey and smoke and whatever else emanates from the strange ancient fortress Lisa envisions as his home.

"Yeah. They're paintings I did over the last 10 or so years. They were just sitting around, so the other night I pulled off the stretchers and folded them into crosses. They serve a purpose this way."

"You didn't feel bad or nothing breaking down all your art?"

"No. I thought about this a lot, and I made all these because art's the only way I've ever been able to express myself, and I think I wanted to just show the world who I was. But it's hard to get people to see it. How many people go to these little galleries? And even the ones that see it, I don't know if they really get it. Not that it matters for art to be effective; it's all in the eye of the beholder and all that, but you know, you kind of want people to get it because then they get you, you know? But maybe that's kind of selfish. Maybe it's not all that important. The world doesn't have to know every single person. There's too many people! Why did I think I was so important? What I do think is important is to contribute. So maybe by folding my square so you can't even see the shape and turning it into something, it obscures my message even more. But it was probably too cryptic for people to get anyway; I don't even know what I was trying to say. I think I said something different in all of them; if you look at them, there really are subtle differences. Like the brushstrokes and the pigment. Some I used a glaze. But that doesn't matter. Now, they're not about me pushing myself onto everyone else; they're about helping everyone, being part of something bigger than myself."

"Be careful thinking like that. Even when you're putting it all on the line for your community, your people, whatever you wanna call it, that can still be a lonely business without real connection. Guess that's why we're sitting here."

The pounding of the nails into the wall is timed so it sounds like rim shots, accentuating Walter's heroism in the face of monsters that seem to Lisa suspiciously like William Blake paintings. The cross separates two Steelers posters, identical down to the IC Light branding, its sharp angles fading into the vignette of the sunless room. Mike frowns at his effort; walks around the bar, his heavy, hot breath like a Blake dragon approaching Lisa; slings the Ikea bag over his shoulder; and returns to the wall.

The second cross attaches, and as he holds a third for placement, Lisa opens her mouth to say these aren't all for him, she still has 22nd through 30th Streets to hit; she can't leave them defenseless. But as the nails pound into the wall, she recalls her neighbor promising she'll hang them later, Ophelia's confusion, the staff at one of the vape shops and their polite thanks before she placed the gift, her work, the culmination of a life devoted to art, on the counter.

As Mike hangs the rest of the contents of the bag, patrons

trickle into the bar. Clay, with his skeletal face and cigarette hanging out of his mouth, could have been painted by Vincent van Gogh. Maurice, another gaunt face behind a faded generic "Pittsburgh Baseball" hat. The demographic for unlicensed local sports gear and half-price well drinks barely after lunchtime. Jodi's friend Alexis, done with her shift as a medical assistant, still in her scrubs. The two young men who come through the door last, Lisa doesn't recognize.

Jodi asks their drink order. A quick look at the taps and the long-haired man replies, "Two Iron Citys." He and his friend, who may regret keeping his thin hair so short when it sheds in the next decade, take obligatory sips of their pints. The long-haired man holds his phone over the complimentary garlic cloves on the bar before pocketing both. He scans his phone over the walls, the garlic bulbs hanging still in their mesh bags. He turns from the bar, focusing his phone on one of the crooked crosses.

Lisa's bag is near empty, and the bar walls are covered with more small crosses than any of those ornate European Gothic cathedrals she admires. The two men, whose presence plunges the average age to somewhere in the late 30s, seem more interested in the decor than the beers they abandon on the bar.

"You like those crosses, the artist's right there." Jodi nods to Lisa.

"Aw shit, you made these?" Mike asks. "You ever think about becoming an artist or something?"

"Or something."

"We're more interested in the garlic," the man with the stubble and the thinning blond hair—Lisa has trouble thinking of him as a man, not a boy, though Jodi checked his ID upon entrance—says. "Like, all the stores are out, and you've got it all here."

His friend, with his long, dark waves looking like they'd flow more naturally over a Victorian collar than a Nike T-shirt, turns his phone toward Mike.

"Gotta protect my customers."

"But isn't this a little excessive? I mean, c'mon. You've got it hanging from the walls, and, literally, everyone else is out."

"Didn't Jodi give you some heads—"

"Cloves," Jodi corrects.

"Cloves, with your beers?"

"Yeah, but that's just a clove. Like, what do I do with that?"

"Keep it in your pocket. Keep vampires away."

"But I gotta buy a drink to get one."

"Could save your life. Plus, you catch a buzz. Seems like a good deal to me."

"Yeah, but like, my old man owns a restaurant, and he needs garlic and can't get it anywhere."

"You wanna shut that camera off and we can talk? I let you two record in here 'cause you were showing how I got the safest place in South Side, but if you wanna talk business, we do that shit off camera."

The talker waves his hand at the documenter, who lowers the phone but doesn't return it to any of the many pockets in his low-slung cargo pants.

"How much is it worth to him, your old man?"

"Dude, are you trying to extort me for garlic? We're just trying to make sure everyone's got what they need to protect themselves."

"Oh, I see what this is." Mike crosses his hand over his chest, the hammer resting in his elbow. If he were posterized, he'd be Soviet "art." Power of the worker. Glory to the worker. "You're a couple communists." Maybe not. "Come in here to try and guilt me into giving away the assets I bought for my business with my forethought. To protect my customers. You think I'm not suffering because all these vampires scaring all my customers out of bars, keeping them rushing home before the sun goes down? Naw, I'm just smart, and I got wise to what they were doing while everyone else 'round here laughed. And now you wanna come take what's mine, put my customers and my business in danger. Get the fuck outta my bar."

"I think we got what we need." The documenter finally speaks.

"You have a lovely day." The talker gives a *Mona Lisa* smirk. Light seeps in the bar with a gas lamp glow as the door swings open.

They're gone, into the waning hours of a gray day, when Jodi speaks. "Good for you, Mike. Next they'll be demanding I split my tips with Curly's down on 10th."

"Like vampires aren't bad enough, now we got communists around here."

Momentary unity against a common foe dissipated, they're alone again. Staring ahead, anywhere but inward. Lost in chatter that's less a conversation and more competing voices, sharing words they need to get out to someone, anyone who will appear to be listening.

Separated by walls not even a shot of Old Crow can break down, alone in their thoughts. Mike ruminating on his declining business. Walter, who knows? Lisa on something niggling the back of her mind . . .

"They're familiars."

"Huh?" Mike lowers the hammer, turns toward Lisa, his latest addition continuing the haphazard Dadaist interior design.

"Familiars. They're a vampire's human helpers. Taking care of daylight things vampires can't handle, bring them victims, keep them safe. They'd want to find out where the bloodsuckers can go without getting staked. A place with garlic and crosses all over the walls and no bouncer to accidentally invite them in is a place they'd want to avoid."

A smack on the bar. Walter rises from his stool, seems to stretch to the ceiling, legs as long as a Dalí elephant's. Muttering, he replaces his bowler hat on his head and shuffles toward the door.

"They better not think of pulling me outta retirement just 'cause I do one surveillance job, wouldn't do a damn thing, wiped my hands of it, not my problem anymore, it if wasn't a goddamn emergency."

"Walter, where are you going?" Jodi frowns.

"You wanna settle up now?" Mike asks.

"I'll be back, just gotta get an eye on these familiars."

"Familiars," Lisa repeats.

"I'm too old for this shit." Walter shakes his head and steps into the gray. The door slams shut with more dramatic effect than his assault on the bar top.

"Shit. Now I gotta worry about that crazy old man," Jodi says.

"How much he owe?" Mike's voice has settled back to inside volume. His eyes stare as if he commands them, not the alcohol demons. He cracks open a Miller High Life to cede back control.

"Twenty-six, but he's good for it."

Lisa slides a $10 bill on the bar and sits her empty pint glass on top.

"You leaving, too?" Mike's champagne of beers is half full. Could be half empty. It doesn't matter. Neither is a good sign.

"Yeah, I gotta get back and walk Koko before the sun goes

down. She's real good at spotting vampires and they're scared of dogs and all, but now that I know about familiars, I'm just not seeing any way to keep us safe when it's dark."

"You need one of these." Again, Mike pulls the axe from among the beer cases under the bar, the blade reflecting in the neon lights.

Lisa moves toward the door, shoves her hand into her purse, her fingers wrapping around the wood that used to hold a piece of her oil on canvas. She raises the stake.

"It's OK. I got this."

THEY DRINK OUR BLOOD

The more Lisa reads, the more she fears. She pulls the leash, urging the 70-pound mutt back in the direction of the old warehouse, but Koko's been cooped up in the studio all day and doesn't realize that daylight is no longer safe. Or has ever been safe. Lisa had been blissfully unaware of familiars, as she was vampires until last week made her afraid of the dark. Now she fears the light as well.

They say ignorance is bliss. In a child's total ignorance, there's no reason to think we can't live forever like the vampire. Until Grandma is in a box looking like a Madame Tussaud and we become aware of cancer. But bliss? Would anyone call it bliss, looking inward, expressing herself on canvas, searching deeper and deeper and finding only another slightly askew orange square? Was she afraid then? Not of monsters, but some inkling that when she peeled back enough layers she'd find nothing at the center?

Maybe. But that thought, if it did exist, never made its way to the canvas. And when Amadeo's closed, when her job evaporated and her paintings returned to her studio and everything that made her an artist was stripped away, it was finally time to look outward to her world. Not van Gogh's window in the asylum. Not Millet's fields. Not Toulouse Lautrec's syphilitic Parisian nightlife. Her world. The world outside her head or whatever it is in her that manifests itself in squares.

The news stole any chance at bliss.

Koko sniffs the sidewalk. To Lisa, it's another agonizing delay before returning to the relative safety of the studio. To Koko, it's more exciting smells. Maybe ignorance could be bliss when you're hardwired to detect threats. When they evolved from the vampire companion wolf, mutating away from the gene that lets vampires assume their shape (as Lisa saw on national news or WTF or TikTok or overheard someone say), dogs must have acquired an extra sense for revenants. Unknown to them, undefined, the flashing danger alarm sounds when a vampire is near.

A young goth, so thin she's almost two-dimensional, struts with determination down the twilit street. Is her skin the pallor of Sargent's *Madame X* because she's been drained by a vampire? Did she give her blood willingly like some groupie, the type of silly woman who writes letters to Richard Ramirez? Or is the ivory white the result of days spent safely locked in a coffin? Or is it true

Pittsburgh is so cloudy the vampires, not just their familiars, can walk among us during the days?

Koko ignores the waif, more intrigued by the malodorous *parfum de gutter*. Lisa remains vigilant, surveying the street, and her heart thrusts itself against her rib cage in a desperate attempt to liberate itself from her chest where it's trapped and confronted with imminent danger. If it could propel from her sternum, shattering ribs, tearing muscle, ripping flesh, it could run the other direction, away from the three boys in the cloud of smoke on the corner.

Even across the street, Lisa can smell what they're smoking. They never drink wine, but do vampires smoke weed? Does their species react to psychedelics, or do they get high on something else? Is high even a concept for them, or is our blood their life *and* their euphoria? We humans always ascribe our own morality to other species, assuming they have the same motivations we do. But how could vampire brains process substances and emotions like we do when they drink our blood?

Lisa tries not to inhale a lungful of the herbal smoke from the shared vape pen while breathing deep enough to slow her heart rate. One of the teenagers, or twenty-somethings (when Lisa turned 40, everyone younger started looking like a kid), in a backward Pirates cap gives a sidelong glance at the dog as they pass; Lisa and Koko are otherwise unnoticed.

"I love you, but that's it for your cavalier attitude today," Lisa mumbles, pulling the leash so Koko walks straight to the warehouse door. "They don't drink your blood unless they're desperate and they've got me right here, and you know I don't have fangs like you do, fangs as big as theirs and a jaw that can rip them apart."

She unlocks the door, and Koko runs into the lobby. "Oh, now you act like you're excited to be home. Why wouldn't you come back earlier? You don't realize it's not safe anymore. Sure, you smell a vampire and your ears perk up and you growl and show what sharp teeth you have and they go running, but what do I do?"

She pulls the elevator grate shut, presses 4.

"I don't have that luxury. I've gotta always be vigilant, wear my silver earrings, hand on my stake. Since no one's inventing a vampire detector anytime soon, I gotta act like they're all vampires. I gotta be prepared."

THEY DRINK OUR BLOOD

She pulls the elevator grate open, and Koko slides across the cool concrete of the hallway toward the heavy studio door. She doesn't have the chomping teeth, the sharp incisors, and the fast-twitch muscle fibers of the dog, so she needs her staple gun, her chisel, her handsaw. She shoves them into the backpack that hangs with her hoodies and a seldom-worn imitation leather jacket on hooks by the door. Her chisel goes in the zipper-front pocket. To pry open a coffin and stake the beast inside? Sure. Her handsaw, wobbly and dull as it is, as she learned making the stake, too dull to sever a vampire head—no matter how ancient and frail and long for blood—in a clean blow like a guillotine, no matter the velocity. But if the vampire already had a stake through its heart and the decapitation was just for insurance . . .

Who is she kidding? Could she ever cut off a head? Saw through flesh, muscle, cartilage, ligaments, tendons, fat, bone, and all the goo and gore and slime that come with it? Hear the tissue ripping? See the viscous innards ooze from their moist containers? Taste the metallic, salty blood that would inevitably turn her face into a sanguinary, monochrome Jackson Pollock piece? Could she be stoic, resist the pleas for mercy, even though she knows they are mere manipulation of her all-too-human empathy?

She's never killed. Except the deer that bolted in front of her car in high school, ending itself and her Oldsmobile Cutlass Supreme. And the spiders and silverfish and stinkbugs that invade the studio. Probably a few sparrows and squirrels that didn't get out of the road when it was either them or her. Or the countless Chinese lanternflies, that invasive species she felt practically deputized to dispatch with Third Reich death machine efficiency as a civic duty.

And isn't that what the vampires are? An invasive species? They may present as humans. They may walk upright, use their opposable thumbs to shift into park and strike a match and summon a ride share. They may speak our languages and buy our real estate and hire us to do their bidding, but they're not human. Their hearts don't beat. Hemoglobin doesn't carry oxygen through their bodies. They're not people; they're not even mammals. Yet they're the top of the food chain.

So why shouldn't she treat them like the mosquito when it lands on her arm and tries to suck her blood?

Next time she leaves the house with silver filament hanging

from her ears and garlic slathered on her wrists like Chanel No. 5, she'll be armed with more than her stake. She'll be a walking fortress, ready to repel and vanquish any enemy.

The Gift beckons from its acrylic case, its heavy iron base ready to sink into a vampire skull, its spikes all but demanding to pierce a throat deeper than even the sharpest vampire fangs. Enough to incapacitate and make her escape.

She moves toward the case atop its white column and stops. Could she let her artifact be covered in blood and gray matter? Or whatever it is that lurks inside the vampires and gives them the appearance of being alive? Could she find a use for Man Ray's purposely useless object?

Could she so oppose the artist's intention? But what was the intention? Surely not to sit in a dirty studio no one visited. Wasn't the point of the movement to be anti-art? To challenge our notions of art? If so, it was never meant to be displayed, but used in a way art never is. And against an existential threat like the world war the Dadaists rallied against.

She stops. It may be worth only a month's rent in the new lofts next door, but that's value. And it's art. Well, anti-art. It's the only object in this lonely room that connects Lisa to the human she thought she was the first 44 years of her life.

Koko stretches out on the couch, so Lisa retreats to the open space she has dedicated to basic living, though it's not sans art. She collapses onto the narrow wooden bed, pressed against the blue wall from which hang four small paintings: a cubist still life, a college acquaintance's self-portrait, impressionist trees abandoned at Amadeo's when the painter OD'd, a portrait of the artist's mother when Lisa was still finding her means of expression back in high school. She'd need to distinguish vampires from the standard angsty, obnoxious, conflicted teenagers so sure of who they were yet so early in their journey to true self-discovery.

She opens the App Store, downloads TikTok.

Account created, she's thrust into a funhouse dystopia where in a split second, she can decide to watch or swipe right past a stranger's life. Bad dancing. Worse dancing. Genetic anomalies. Artificial anomalies. All that's missing is the Fiji mermaid.

Visible rib cages right into fat rolls in places even Rubens couldn't imagine. And monologues—were they truly extemporaneous, or did the liminal space setting just imply it?—

some seemingly apropos of nothing, others responding to a little dialogue bubble with a user name, giving Lisa the experience of joining a conversation midway. It was like sidling up to hip attendees at a gallery opening, ready to join their joy, discuss the works on display, whatever was making them laugh and smile. If she commented on the video, would the response be an emoji of a strained smile, a pitying gaze, a tacit reminder that she was just the help?

More dancing.

No vampires.

She opens Facebook, scrolls through the group posts, ignoring the pleas to visit Jake's Mistake until she sees the video about the familiars, the one that first propelled her into this kaleidoscope of decontextualized glimpses of a species in jeopardy.

She taps the creator's username, hits follow, peruses her videos. How to write a blog with generative AI. How to read faster. How to hack the algorithm for more views. Back in the "How to spot a familiar" video, she pulls up the caption and taps #vampire.

Silliness. Capes, fanged face filters. Back to the familiar video, she tries again: #vampiresarereal.

She becomes one of the 800K viewers of the first video on the grid, of what appear to be seven teenagers in low-slung, acid-washed jeans and T-shirts, gazing down at votive candles on a sidewalk arranged to spell "Die." The flames illuminate the spray-painted words on the cement: "Fuck you and all of you."

The text on the screen asks, "WTH?"

The comments answer: "Vampire ritual." "They're telling us their plans." "They're not even bothering to hide anymore."

In the next video, a masked but helmetless rider speeds past cars on a bridge while balancing on the back wheel of what Lisa's always heard called a crotch rocket. The title: "Vampires or teenagers?"

The first 10 or so of the 700 comments were split. Some said it didn't matter: "Both are out to destroy and nothing else." "Who cares? Stake them all!"

Lisa's next swipe summons a woman with the lifted skin, jutting cheekbones, plumped lips, and cat eyes of one who may want to become a vampire simply for its anti-aging benefits. The woman blinks, and her eyelashes detach. Oh, it's a filter. In the green screen behind her is an online news article.

"So, I wanted to share this story because I don't think y'all have seen it yet since it's being buried by everyone who wants us to remain calm and act like vampires don't exist." She air-quotes these last three words with acrylic Nosferatu nails. "Basically, high-ranking vampires met and discussed their ongoing plans to dominate the world and feed off the human race. A recording of the event leaked and RT broke it. So, of course, since it's from a 'bad country', all our networks and news outlets are blocking it. Even though there's evidence of a massive conspiracy that puts our entire existence at risk."

The video cuts and starts autoplaying from the beginning. Lisa scrolls past and keeps scrolling into the abyss, her eyelids failing before her fingers.

THEY DRINK OUR BLOOD

When the morning WTF News broadcast reports a man found dead in a clawfoot tub in the South Side, an artist's first thought is the *Death of Marat* by Jacques-Louis David. Blood seeps from the chest wound through the towel covering the modest revolutionary as he all but spills from his green tub. In one hand a quill, the other still clutches the list of citizens who would soon be separated from their heads. One dead so thousands may live.

The victim of the "apparent stabbing" is male, and the tub isn't filled with water for bathing but soil to grow plants that, if not dead from the frost, would surely be a second victim under the deadweight of the first.

Lisa can't work today. It's not safe. Not even dropping off someone's chicken with garlic sauce if she were to finally start using her car for food delivery as the ride-share app email marketing messages urged. Who heard of fending off a vampire with fragrant Chinese takeout?

WTF News says nothing of where on the body the stabbing occurred. Was it the femoral artery? So close to the groin, that would be in keeping with the prurient nature of these vampires she fell asleep learning about last night. They prefer this artery due to its aggressive blood flow and proximity to the life-giving organs of humans, almost as though it fortifies the blood with even more nutrients for whatever it is the vampire considers life. Sexually humiliating to the victim, it would feel appropriately intimate for a bathtub murder, albeit a bathtub that was serving as a planter on a sidewalk.

While the news divulges few details, Lisa's mind fills in the blanks with the victim's head lolling, hanging on by threadlike tendons, the flesh shredded as if the attacker bit in a ravenous frenzy. The attacker is Magritte's *Young Girl;* the male victim of an undisclosed age is the bird being eaten. With the neck snapped at the bone, the shoulder is the only reason the head doesn't roll onto the sidewalk and provide exciting new smells for Koko's next walk.

If there would be a next walk.

The sky could be clear and sunlit, but the South Side streets will be nocturnal as long as this nightmare persists. Yet another Magritte comes to mind: *Empire of Light*, in which the blue sky is a surreal contrast to the night scene below. Koko will have to accept the sidewalk, no more than arm's length from the building's front door.

She's not happy with Lisa tugging on her leash, walking up the steps and across each floor of the warehouse as her exercise after just enough time to fill a bag outside. She barks in protest on the third ascent.

If Koko could kick and scream, she would do so as Lisa drags the restless dog back into the studio. Pulling shut the heavy door leaves her lightheaded. Koko follows her to the kitchenette. Dog food is in abundance in the pantry of this space cobbled together from other people's garbage; human food is not. For a moment, she considers ordering delivery. The moment passes. Does placing an order count as an invitation to enter?

She can't risk it. Lisa pulls a can of Campbell's tomato soup from a cabinet.

This is not sustainable. She'll have to leave eventually. War kills just as much by starvation as by bullets and bombs. She can ration, but first she must secure the rations to ration. And before that, she must learn everything else about the latest atrocity.

The Facebook group has been active this morning.

At 8:43 a.m., Mike Carloni posted, "Jake's Mistake is open! Bring your breakfast sammy and wash it down with a Miller Lite. Take home your FREE garlic clove well before the sun sets!"

The tomato soup concentrate plops into the two-cup saucepan on the camper-size stove. Everything in this studio has an air of transience. Gaps in the mismatched, makeshift cabinetry in this section of the spacious room that Lisa decided decades ago would be her kitchen remind her of another job not completed. The bedroom is only partially enclosed with two boards of drywall, a respite no more permanent than van Gogh's stay in the mental institution that apparently had much better views than the weeds and train tracks outside Lisa's window. Or he just had more imagination, more talent. Maybe to him, weeds and train tracks looked like *Starry Night*. Maybe that's why he's considered a genius. And maybe that's why he was in the loony bin in the first place.

Lisa was never supposed to stay here, not for more than a decade. She was supposed to evolve. And she has. What surroundings she'd grown into, she still doesn't know.

THEY DRINK OUR BLOOD

She fills the Campbell's can with water from the single-basin sink, its white plastic construction tinted with paint from washing her brushes where she washes her dishes.

Lisa has evolved; her habitat hasn't. When she applied for the studio and the subsidy that came with it 20 years ago, she was a young artist. She wasn't starving with the income from the school photography gig, but she wasn't any higher on the societal ladder than van Gogh's *Potato Eaters*. Food didn't matter. Art was her sustenance. Like a vampire subsisting on blood, Lisa lived on creating. Her oxygen was oil paint and turpentine fumes.

It doesn't satiate her anymore.

Maybe it hasn't for a long time. Maybe even before Amadeo's closed. Maybe she was just lying to herself because she was too scared to do something else. What is she qualified to do besides deliver food and people and the occasional vampire to their destinations? So she stayed, kept painting the same squares until they stacked up uselessly on her table. They were pointless . . . until she converted them to vampire shields.

And that could be where this ennui is originating. Her purpose served no purpose. What does art do in an existential crisis? How can a painting save a life? When fangs are at your throat, a Calder mobile isn't going to save you. When vampires infiltrate and pervert every institution in our society to cater to their nefarious goals, what's a *Nude Descending a Staircase* going to do to thwart their protocols? When they subjugate us all, keep us alive only in the most literal sense to feed on our blood, no triptych is coming to the rescue.

The artist must finally set aside the decadence of decorative creation and join the anonymous mass of resistance. The art must become a weapon. And not a weapon of changing minds, a real weapon.

The soup is better as art than as a meal. Maybe it looks too much like the blood she imagines spewing from the faceless, nameless victim posed like Marat. Maybe she's finally lost her taste for starving-artist food. She needs a distraction.

Up in Ithaca, two college sophomores have been arrested for what the anchor calls the Big Red Blood Drain. The girls with their black hair, dead eyes, ruby lips, and *Venus de Milo* complexions are not staying in the shadows. They're emboldened, too sure of their diabolical power to remain hidden any longer. No jail will hold these two, not with their bloodsucking, parasitic species having infiltrated the fundamental institutions that were supposed to be for the People, not these interlopers loyal to neither nation nor flesh.

She flips to WTF News. The five-day weather forecast may as well come from tea leaves. Unless vampires melt in water like green witches, the evening rain should no longer count as news.

"Now, breaking news. Police have released the name of the victim in the South Side bathtub death. Retired parking authority employee Walter Givens, whose residence we are told was mere blocks from where he was found, has been found dead of an apparent stabbing."

When the photo appears on screen, Lisa goes deaf. As it appears to be a city employee ID photo, he is without his bowler hat, and his eyes, usually with lids at half-mast after hours at Jake's, are wide open. Sober, alert on screen. Dead in a bathtub. Off to hunt familiars. He got too close. They'll stop at nothing to enslave us.

In the deepest depths of the subconscious that only Dalí or Max Ernst explored, she knows she flicked on the TV hoping it would all be over, that some man with a chiseled jaw and a mustache would tell her vampires are not real. It was all a big misunderstanding. Go back to sleep, America. Oh, the comfort of being insane. She'd be safer if the monsters were inside her head, though maybe no less anxious and melancholy.

That man with the mustache doesn't exist. There is no bearer of good news. All messengers must be killed. If for no other reason than their complacency. You're all doomed. Now here's Jim with sports.

On her phone, Lisa opens Facebook.

The first post, right at the top of her feed; she doesn't need to navigate to the group to see it. The group has come to her, posted five minutes ago.

Autumn Mallory: Neighbors! For those of you who haven't seen the news, we lost a member of our community today. I'm sure you've seen Walter Givens around the neighborhood. The photo below is what the news is showing, but you probably know him by his distinct hat and caring nature. I'm organizing a benefit tonight for Walter to raise money for his funeral expenses and I'm looking for a venue. Anyone willing to host?

THEY DRINK OUR BLOOD

Lisa expands the comments.

Mike: You're welcome at Jake's Mistake! Walter was a regular and we're grieving hard here. We're open now and happy to host!

Autumn Mallory: Perfect! I'm thinking 4 pm.

Mike: Good deal. We're open now, so if any of yinz can't wait til 4, stop down!

Autumn: Thank you!

Five hours until the benefit. Five hours before Lisa has something to do, something to occupy her mind, to get it to stop contorting itself. She can't work, can't trust strangers without seeing their reflections or knowing they haven't been seduced by the power of the bloodthirsty revenants, can't trust herself. What would she do if another passenger disappeared in the rearview? Would she grab her stake, fling off her seat belt, and launch herself over the center console and start stabbing—only to find he'd just leaned over to tie his shoe?

She could go to Jake's early. They're open. That means hours potentially alone with Mike. Is that really so bad? Maybe last week, but there's some comfort in drunken, lecherous looks. At least what he's hungry for isn't blood. He and Lisa are the same kind: the hunted. Prey need to stick together, form a pack for strength in numbers.

She'll go after showering, shaving her legs, washing her newly cut hair.

The Lisa that emerges after 90 minutes isn't so much a woman as a masterwork personified. White button-down loose over black pleather leggings, black boots with a chunk of a heel, black imitation leather jacket dusted off from where it hung for months, circuit board earrings. She slings the backpack over one shoulder and wraps the leash around her left wrist where, in another life, a silver bracelet might have been. In her right hand, she clutches *The Gift*. The Dada object feels like her next evolution, making her hand a clockwork orange with nails sharper than Nosferatu's.

I am become art.

THEY DRINK OUR BLOOD

The Man Ray rides shotgun. Koko and the backpack full of makeshift weapons take the back seat.

With parking fees waived before drinking hours to entice more people to explore the exciting, fun, zero-proof attractions of the South Side, Lisa beats the odds as she slides the HHR right in front of Jake's. It's sadly ironic that Walter would have nothing to enforce these days.

Inside the bar are the regulars she expects three hours before the party starts. Clay, the smoke-sucking skeleton, and two retirees still observing their post-third-shift shot-and-a-beer, though the last time they clocked out from the plant was years ago. Replace all three with coffins, and the energy would stay the same.

Even when they're not sucking your blood, vampires are draining the life from a bar, a neighborhood, a city, and, if they're not stopped, a world.

For a moment, Koko brings life into the dark room. Clay's eyes open wide, and he beckons the dog to come over. Lisa pulls her leash fast.

"What do you think you're doing bringing a dog in here?" Mike's voice is stable, his words as clear as his words in the Facebook comments. It's early yet.

"She's here for protection. Dogs are vampires' sworn enemies. With their keen sense of smell, they can detect a vampire well before we can. And I dunno, but vampires are afraid of them."

"That's not what I read. I read vampires summon wolves or turn themselves into wolves and dogs are descendants of wolves, so they're basically vampires on four legs."

"Well, I've seen Koko chase vampires through the South Side when they tried to seduce me into letting them drink my blood last weekend, and I know she's got more Van Helsing in her than vampire."

"OK, whatever." Mike walks behind the bar, pops a Miller High Life. "Who knows what to believe anymore?"

"Maybe that's what they want, to make us all confused. Maybe they use it as a weapon," Jodi says.

"Yeah, yeah, yeah, yeah. They've been around thousands of years making up stories about themselves. Turning into mist. You hear that shit?"

"Making it so crazy and supernatural we don't want to believe they exist, so they hide in plain sight." Lisa stares into the Straub draft Jodi slid in front of her without asking, as if the foggy pint glass and its rising sediment hold her future.

"Fucking devil shit. So the dog's gonna protect us, huh?"

"Her name's Koko."

"I'd rather her name be Killer or some shit, but if you say she protects us, I trust you. Maker of all these crucifixes won't steer me wrong."

"Crosses," Lisa mutters too softly for Mike to hear as he takes his beer to the bathroom.

"Coco, huh?" Jodi emerges from behind the bar and kneels down as if to inspect the dog. "Like Chanel?"

"No, like Mark Rothko. He was an abstract painter. When I was in seventh grade, I knew I wanted to be an artist. I was already taking classes and entering contests, and one class I took did a trip up to New York to the museums. The MOMA, Museum of Modern Art, and hanging on the white wall is this huge canvas. And it's just colors. Not any pattern, no clean lines, no subject matter at all to speak of. Just one sort of weird, ragged square shape, but not a shape, just how the paint manifested itself. And another one, a little smaller, above it, divided by another, I guess, area of color. It's the type of art that people who don't know art think their kid could do, but people who know art understand is a masterpiece. I still had so much to learn about art, but even at 12, I got it.

"And I didn't just see it or even feel it. I experienced it. Like how people talk about God. I had that with that untitled canvas. It surrounded me. I was rolling in the waves of color. I could hear it. Like those synesthesia folks. I could hear, smell, taste, feel it, even though it was only coming in my eyes. It wasn't any emotion that has a name. You can't put that feeling in words. Only art can express it. And that's what I've been trying to do for the past 30 years. And I failed. If I hadn't, you'd all be staring so hard at those crosses you'd know they're not crucifixes. That's how I know they're better like that. If art doesn't transfix and, like, abduct you into its world, is it even art or just something that hangs on the wall?"

Silence. A cough from deep in Clay's black lungs. Jodi looks into Lisa's eyes, looks away, looks back into her eyes, and asks, "You see the news about Ithaca?"

"Oh. Oh, yeah. Those girls don't even try to hide they're vampires, do they?"

"They'll be out by morning."

"How do you figure? It looked to me like the Ithaca people were sure they had the right criminals and they'd be keeping them."

"No way the rich vampires are letting those girls get exposed to sunlight in lockup. Not with the lawyers vampires have. I wouldn't be surprised if vampires were secretly running the district attorney's office."

"You know, I was just thinking how we haven't heard any updates on the Denning case. High-profile, you know? It made national news. And nothing from the city. No charges, no suspects even. You think with all the news coverage, there'd be some pressure to solve it."

"That's what I mean. They've been pulling the strings all along."

"No one ever sees justice."

It's not until Autumn enters the bar—with an empty Costco-sized clear plastic pretzel barrel that she says is for donations—that the dearly departed for whom they are all gathered here is mentioned.

"So, you knew Walter?" Mike asks, smoothing his thinning hair, throwing his shoulders back, trying to shed the past 10 years.

"Walter was my hero! Seriously, he saved my ass three times in this skeezy part of town with his karate."

"Walter?" Mike laughs. "He actually knew karate?"

"I dunno if it was karate or one of those other martial arts, but when this creep recognized me from the club and started shouting 'Rhoda!' and chasing me out the bar, thinking he could put his hands all over me just 'cause no big bouncers were around, Walter sure as hell knew something that scared him off."

"The club?" Mike hasn't sipped his beer since the Jane Avril with the lash extensions and crop top entered the bar, hasn't fixated on Koko, hasn't focused his beady eyes on Lisa, making her feel like she's in a tub of slithering maggots, hasn't revealed whether the demon always lurking in his brain has yet been summoned to command him.

"Tinsel Cowgirl."

The strip club. Mike smiles. Jodi rolls her eyes and refills Lisa's beer.

Lisa opens TikTok, scrolls past any video without captions. She catches a few words of Mike and Autumn's conversation. Hero. Saved me from some asshole. Hero. Probably went out trying to save someone. Figures vampires don't take the handsy creeps that deserve it.

Lisa delves into that handheld multiverse, slipping from one reality to another at a rapid clip. She's in a kitchen, learning how to create cologne from garlic, then in a classroom for the anatomy lesson, detailing the exact point on the neck to cut when you need to sever a head from a body.

A woman staring from an undisclosed location with the caption, "When you find out vampires exist and it explains all the evil in the world."

A man wears the same expression beneath the caption, "When you find out vampires exist and it explains all the r@pe, murd3r, cruelty, and greed in the world."

"When you find out vampires exist and it explains all that is evil."

"When you find out vampires exist and it explains everything."

"When you find out vampires exist and it explains my dad."

"When you find out vampires exist and it explains all that causes pain."

"When you find out vampires exist and it explains why we can't heal."

"When you find out vampires exist and it explains all that is evil."

"When you find out vampires exist and it explains all that is evil."

"When you find out vampires exist and it explains everything stopping us from being happy."

"When you find out vampires exist and it explains all that is evil."

"When you find out vampires exist and it explains all that is evil."

"When you find out vampires exist and it explains all that is evil."

"When you find out vampires exist and it explains all that is evil."

Lisa puts down her phone. It explains why Walter will never get the justice he deserves.

THEY DRINK OUR BLOOD

Even when other conversations drown out Mike and Autumn's and loose change weighs down the pretzel barrel, it explains why this collection, this benefit will never be enough to fix their world.

"Well, if it isn't the thirsty dog."

Lisa turns in her stool to see that the expert in vampire lore has left the Bat Cave for Jake's this afternoon. He's accompanied by a slight, also dark-haired man—both around Lisa's age but clearly never having taken six months off from self-care.

"She's more a bodyguard than a barfly. I don't know how many vampires she's saved me from since Saturday night, but I bet it's a lot with how often she likes to be walked and how far she goes and—"

"Right." Hank bends down to rub Koko on the head then turns away, devoting all his attention to the bar, suddenly desperate for a drink.

The door swings open again, and a hulking figure in a bomber jacket becomes a silhouette in the doorway.

"Hank!" the man says.

"Thor." Oh right, Lisa remembers: the local celebrity detective that was filling in as a bouncer when that actor was acting entitled the night before he found out he was as vulnerable as the rest of us to the vile bloodsuckers.

"Hank, you are the last person I'd've thought I'd see here tonight."

"You'd be less surprised to see David Hockney?"

"Sure. He could be doing some Pop Art retrospective at the Warhol Museum. I hear famous folks like to come down here."

"If Hockney came to the bar you were bouncing, would you card him?"

"Well, he is about 87 now—" Lisa turns to the two men standing behind her, but they fail to notice her interjection.

"Sheee-it, maybe just to see if it were really him, not one of those kids from the SFX school showing off. But, seriously, Hank, you're at a benefit?"

"Alex says we're 'part of a community.'" Hank air-quotes, shaking his head.

"That's damn right!" The man who drapes his arms over Hank's shoulders is smaller, wispier, younger. He attaches himself as if they are a single unit and only allotted a particular amount of space. "We participate now. We don't just lurk."

"Alex is on the neighborhood council," Hank says.

"And I give Hank five years before he joins, too," Alex says.

Thor laughs, shakes his head, orders a Pabst from Jodi. "So, either of you know the deceased?"

"You working the case, Thor?"

"Nah, man. At least not yet. No one's called asking for an investigation, not with the cops on it. But they dig up nothing, we'll see. Just wondering's all."

"I'd know him to see him. You don't see a lot of bowler hats these days," Hank says. "Now, one less."

"I met him once. The man talked my head off with some crazy story about fighting monsters," Alex says.

"What about you, Thor?"

"Sheee-it, feels like I'm the only one down here who remembers him as a parking enforcer. Wrote me a $200 ticket."

"Handicap spot?"

"Nah, I parked down at the public pay lot on 18th back when I was bouncing at Snaps. Crew stayed on after shift, and I got blitzed and walked home."

"Responsible."

"That's what I say! Problem is they block the lot the next morning for the farmer's market. I come down to get it, and there's my big-ass beater with a crate of tomatoes on the hood and a whole tent colony set up around it."

Hank and Alex laugh. Lisa smiles in spite of the tragedy, in spite of the conversation happening behind her, without her. She may as well be furniture. Not some Mae West lip sofa, more like a switch-plate cover that doesn't quite match the paint.

"Walter stood there all day, adding ticket after ticket because— wild shit—I still hadn't moved the car."

"The most shocking part about that story," Alex says, "is that the South Side used to have a farmer's market."

"And will again, with you on the council." Hank rubs his partner's shoulder, sips his whiskey. "Much to my chagrin."

The three keep talking, laughing, behind her, every so often scratching Koko behind her ears before resuming discussions of neighborhood nightlife. Thor's recent case involving a car with flat tires and a baseball bat, the new menu at the Bat Cave, the upcoming performance of the drag queen Kristal Nacht at the MaleBox. Lisa picks up snippets of the conversations of strangers who drop in barely long enough to drop a dollar in the pretzel barrel. She watches the regulars stare into their shot glasses as if their escape into their drinks could be permanent, shrinking themselves into an entire world existing in a 1.5-ounce cup that can't be worse than the full-size one they're in.

Eventually the Bat Cave regulars disappear, and the conversation—the life of the bar—silences. The only sounds are the whistles and creaks that make the old building seem haunted and Sublime's "Badfish" playing softly when Clay says, "Shouldn't someone make a speech?"

Slumped behind the bar, Mike belches, "About what?"

"Walter," Autumn says. "Right?"

"Yeah."

After a moment of silence due to lack of words instead of dedication, Clay continues, "Me? Nah, I'm not a word man."

"Walter was . . . " Jodi says, purses her lips, opens her mouth, closes it again, before finally saying, "Walter was."

"I'll drink to that!" The bearded biker—who appeared sometime around when the sun had moved far enough to the west that most customers were closing their tabs—does drink to it, downs his beer, and slams the glass on the bar.

"You better drink another one to him, Wolf." Jodi swipes his empty pint glass and takes it back to the beer tap.

"Fuck yeah, I will. And you know what? Shots all around! Walter would've wanted it that way. On me."

Jodi grabs a plastic handle of Vladimir from the bottom shelf, pours the rotgut vodka Lisa hasn't seen since freshman year in college into shot glasses, and distributes one each in the general vicinity of Wolf, Mike, Autumn, Clay, and Lisa.

"To Walter," Wolf says. "Crazy fucker."

The heavy-bottomed glasses patter on the bar, a millisecond out of sync. They return empty at greater intervals. There's an involuntary near-gag from Lisa as the vodka burns her throat until she washes it down with beer that's as flat as a medieval painting before they understood perspective. Then silence, or what passes in a bar for silence.

"Shit. I thought people were s'posed to be thirsty on Thursdays," Mike says.

"I'm thirsty!" Wolf pounds his fist on the bar. It comes away wet. "Another round for all of us. You too, sweetheart." He winks at Jodi.

"DK days. Thursdays were our party nights. Whole campus knew us. Thursday night: You know where your girlfriend is?"

Jodi hands Mike his new shot. He downs it. No toast this time. The rest of the patrons follow.

"Our parties wouldn't even start till 10. Where's everybody at? What time is it?"

"Eight forty-two," Autumn says.

"Eight forty-two! I tell you where they are," Mike says. "They're all at home, hiding from the fucking vampires bleeding us to the bone. It's 10 o'clock you don't know where your girlfriend is, she's in an alley with some filthy fangs in her neck. And we're all going broke because of it."

Jodi nods. "Amen to that. No customers, no tips."

"I can't pick up riders if I don't know they're not vampires. I had one this week."

"Vampire?" Autumn asks.

Lisa nods. "He was right in my back seat, but I couldn't see him in the mirror. I haven't taken any riders since then. How can I? Can't risk picking up any more vampires. What if one of them is so hungry he'll risk my silver earrings? I can't even deliver food, not since Akron and those familiars luring a driver—"

"What? I didn't seen that one. Mike, you gotta let me turn on the news here again. I don't care it's depressing; it's our reality!"

"I saw it on TikTok," Lisa says.

Autumn shakes her head. "No wonder the other girls won't come in to work nights. I thought they were crazy. Who wants lunch shift at a strip club? I guess I gotta follow the news. Aside from those couple incidents with assholes and Walter saving me, I never felt all that in danger down here. Like, it's kinda shitty, but not dangerous. At least not until Walter died. I guess I should have been paying attention."

"He didn't die. He got murdered," Jodi says. "Keep that in your head, and you'll start being scared like you should be."

"I ain't scared," Wolf says. "They've been hiding for thousands of years for a reason. They're the ones scared of us. We go around acting all terrified of them, we give 'em power. Gotta bring back the way it was. Make 'em scared to come out at night because the people are out with their torches and pitchforks."

"Damn, that's good. Get down to Jake's Mistake, or the vampires win." Mike pulls his phone from his pocket, swipes to unlock the screen. "If the vampires are keeping them home, it's like. It's like . . . "

"Like they're dead already," Lisa says.

"That's even better." Mike thrusts his beer overhead, bathing the bar with foam in celebration of Lisa's witticism, which will no doubt be lost from the ethanol to the ether before he can open Facebook, find the Down Low group, start a post, and transcribe it without typos. He makes it through the first two steps when his marble eyes go wide at the tiny screen.

"What is it, Mike?" Jodi approaches him.

Lisa opens Facebook, navigates to the group. Upon seeing the video at the top, she knows what Mike's drunken eyes are trying to decipher.

Lisa reads, "Hey, South Side. My security cam caught the murder victim last night, I'm posting the footage here as I showed it to the police and they didn't seem all that concerned. They didn't tell me to keep it secret or anything, so I figured I'd post it here to see if anyone recognized any of the other people with him and anyway, A.C.A.B."

Forgetting her audience, she clicks the video. Autumn watches over her shoulder. There goes Walter, immortal in pixelation. Lisa blinks away the film the vodka left on her eyes. It takes a second for her to recognize the tall figure in the camera distortion without his bowler hat, and by that point, he's disappeared off-screen.

"Give me your phone." Jodi snatches the device from Mike's hand. "You're not even in the right app anymore."

"Damn buttons are too small for my fingers. I got big hands," he says, staring at Autumn. If she's impressed by his implication—and his nose that seems to expand and redden as his eyes shrink to black caviar—she doesn't let on as she remains fixated on the tiny video.

A couple of seconds pass before what appears to be a bell-bottomed hippie walks through, followed by a near-knee-length Biggie Smalls T-shirt capped with a bowler hat, and a lanky figure in a hoodie stretching as high on screen as Walter had.

The video stops, the whole procession lasting less than 20 seconds.

"Well, I can see why the cops aren't making much of this. Dressing up in their parents' clothes has never been illegal." Jodi hands the phone back to Mike.

"Or maybe those are their clothes, and they've been wearing them for 30 years. Maybe they're locked forever in the time they were turned." Lisa hits "play" again.

"Oh! Of course!" Autumn says. "They'd want to stay in the last moments they were really alive."

Jodi rips the phone back out of Mike's hand. "See the guy in the huge shirt; doesn't that look like Walter's hat?"

"Yeah . . . "

As the gaunt figure in the hoodie lopes into the screen, Lisa pauses the video.

"What are you seeing?" Autumn asks. "He got anything of Walter's?"

"Just his blood. Oh, my God. That's him. That's the vampire."

"The vampire? Lemme see!" Mike snatches his phone back from Jodi. "Which one?"

"The tall one. That's the thing that was in my car."

"I thought you couldn't see him."

"Not in the mirrors, but I saw his photo in the app. And that hoodie. And just like that, when he walked away from my car to . . . I know where they are."

"The vampires?" Jodi leaves Mike and his phone to approach Lisa.

"Yes. I know where their—" she pauses, searching for the word buried in the fathoms of Straub pints and vodka shots until the tide unfurls and it spills from her mouth. "Their lair is."

Mike jumps from his stool, slams his bottle on the bar. It's empty. "Then we better get the fuck down there and let the bloodsucking vermin know they're not welcome here."

"And how do we do that?" Jodi asks.

"Torches and pitchforks."

"Aw, c'mon, Wolf. You know we don't have those."

"No, but we have this." Lisa places her handcrafted wooden stake on the bar.

The butt of Wolf's bowie knife, its blade concealed in leather like Wolf himself, makes a more menacing sound when struck on the bar. He removes the sheath, and its blade gleams red under the neon Coors Light sign.

"That for fighting vampires?" Jodi asks.

"That's for fighting anyone trying to push me around and hold me down."

"I got this!" Cigarette dangling from his lips that almost appear to be receding into his face like a living voodoo experiment, Clay raises his walking cane. Twisting off the plastic topper carved like a crude imitation crystal reveals a blade. It's smaller, thinner, less lustrous, and duller than Wolf's, but suddenly makes Clay less decrepit, though no more lustrous.

Any gawking at Clay's revelation is cut short by smashing glass and Koko's frantic barking. Mike raises the remains of his beer bottle in its new random, angular half-cylinder.

"You can't take that!" Jodi reaches to pry the bottle from his hand and thinks better of it.

"Why not? It's as sharp as Wolf's blade. One of our pledges needed 27 stitches when he sliced his leg with one of these at our dressed-to-get-laid party."

"That's exactly why you can't have it." Jodi stares him down, but Mike clutches the bottle, his eyes tiny beads of moon rock.

"They drink our blood, Jodi! You gotta take anything that'll keep them away."

It's not until Autumn asks, "You cut yourself, wouldn't it be like blood in the water to a shark? A vampire wouldn't be able to control himself?"

"She's right," Jodi says. "We need weapons that'll save us, not hurt us."

"If we're gonna drive them out of town, we gotta show them we know what they are. Torches and pitchforks are scary to us, but you can't cut a head off with a pitchfork. You kill a vampire by staking it through the heart, chopping its head off, and lighting it on fire. We bring things to do that, they'll know we're not being fooled. We know the truth. They're here. They been here all along; they just convinced us they didn't exist. We bring crosses, too, and garlic. And we show them South Side is no place for vampires." Wolf sheaths his bowie knife in punctuation.

Koko snarfles, already asleep again after the shattering glass. Otherwise, the bar is silent.

"I was just messing with yinz." Mike grins. He reaches under the bar. Lisa knows what's coming, but unlike just yesterday, she feels reassured when she sees the axe. It's what surgery to remove this vampire cancer deserves.

"That's more like it," Wolf says. "They'll know we're ready to cut off a head."

"I've got more in my car," Lisa says.

Lisa cuts the engine in the abandoned, overgrown parking lot on an unnamed street behind the abandoned, overgrown Nova Metals building where she dropped off the vampire, the locations separated by abandoned, overgrown industrial buildings.

"Why we all the way back here?" Mike's volume would be more appropriate from the back of a bus, not the front passenger seat of the HHR. The garlic stench is so nauseating Lisa wonders for a moment if she's becoming a vampire.

"I didn't want them to hear Wolf's bike." The throttling that's followed them since departing Jake's Mistake has finally silenced.

"Without surprise, we don't have much advantage," Autumn says from the back seat, clearly visible in the rearview as she strokes Koko's head.

"Not with their superhuman strength."

"But they don't have this!" Mike's arm flings up from the floor between his legs, nearly delivering an unwanted gift to the window. "What the fuck is this?" He lowers *The Gift*, examining it as a utilitarian object, not a Dadaist statement.

"It's a Man R—it's mine." Lisa reaches out her hand.

"It's too heavy for you. I'll be taking it in."

"You've already got an axe, Mike."

At the tap on the window, Lisa silences a scream. The back door opens.

"I'm not letting them go without us." Clay pulls himself out of the car. Lisa opens her mouth to say they're not going anywhere, that Jodi and Wolf don't know where they're going, that even though they don't need an invitation, knocking on doors of abandoned buildings will likely prove fruitless.

"But, like, won't that thing just confuse the vampires anyway? Not scare them?" Autumn asks.

"Someone came swinging that over his head, it'd scare me." Mike attempts to swing it over his head. The ceiling interferes.

"Yeah, but you're human. Aren't vampires superhuman?"

"Subhuman," Lisa says. "But they do have super strength. *The Gift* wouldn't be a real threat to them. They'd know it wouldn't get deep enough to stab their hearts or even—"

"Plus, I think men with axes are kinda sexy in a lumberjack way," Autumn says.

"OK, whatever. You take it. But I still think you're lying, and it's some sort of magic vampire det . . . det . . . keeper offer that you're not telling me."

Lisa accepts *The Gift* just as she did when Camille gave it to her back in March and death-grips the handle. Maybe it's magic. Maybe vampires hate Dada as much as Hitler did.

Lisa steps out of the car, opens the back driver's-side door, liberates Koko so far as the leash will allow. She pops the trunk and slips her backpack full of all the unclaimed art supplies over her shoulders.

A distant rumble quickly transforms into a clatter, and the cratered asphalt with weeds sprouting from the cracks that had moments ago felt solid shakes beneath her feet. With a thundering racket, the earth opens its sharp-toothed mouth, sucking her six feet down into the wooden box stinking of decay, splintered where an undead preternaturally strong hand busted through the planks with black belt finesse, escaping the natural fate of absorbing into the earth, recycling into the planet, feeding new life, to instead last forever a scourge on humanity, like a plastic bag that has made its way out to sea to strangle turtles, suffocate coral, and drain the life from the natural order.

The train passes, and the lot is silent again, except that Autumn is speaking. Lisa looks up from the decrepit yet functionally intact pavement into the green eyes behind the false lashes.

"Since you have your . . . your thing now, I was hoping I could take the stake. I just feel a lot more comfortable with it ,and I think you know a lot more about vampires than I do."

"You want my stake?"

"Yeah, I mean, I think I should have it, right? Seeing how you got your iron thing back with my help and all."

"Yeah, OK. That's fine." Lisa twists, thrusting her hip to the younger woman as her hands are occupied with a dog and a Dada object. "Grab it out of my waistband."

They walk to the opposite end of the lot. The side they enter abuts a road and office complex which, although empty for the night, is not the nothingness past the cement partition. Their motion is righteous, and any officer in his right mind would be on their side in this existential battle, but six adults with booze on their breath and armed with axes and art might still raise suspicion. Their garlic stench is the only way to identify them as Van Helsings, not Renfield-level lunatics.

In the darkness, they stumble over detritus of abandonment, but no one falls. As they exit the lot and step over the old trolley tracks that have been absorbed into the blacktop, Lisa's throat clenches.

Do the others feel it, too? Do they have to make a conscious effort to exhale? Has the automatic nervous system become an effort? Clay limps, lagging behind Autumn's practiced strut, Wolf's Neanderthal gait. Mike carries the axe on his shoulder like a lumberjack who, with one step into one of the myriad potholes, could give himself the van Gogh makeover. Only Jodi looks back at Lisa, waiting for Koko to finish her business on the rocky pavement.

Sorry, neighbors. She has no free hand for bagging. A little organic biohazard is the least of anyone's concerns. And she has to keep moving forward. Any hesitation and her pounding heart may win the battle against her brain, and she'll be back in the car, driving away from the vampires.

The way she sees it, she has three options. Pretend, like the local authorities, that vampires don't exist, that everything is fine, keep calm and carry on, nothing to see here. Chernobyl is just having a technical difficulty. Or she could hide like so many of her neighbors and let the South Side be drained of its lifeblood, its people. She may as well give her neck to a vampire.

Or she could be part of the solution.

She accelerates, Koko nearly reaching a gallop to assume the lead as they round the corner onto the road Lisa knows as Kishinev Street from her ride-share GPS, but no one has bothered to label. It's wide enough for four lanes between the loading docks on the right and the administrative buildings being gradually engulfed by nature on the left.

Approaching the ramshackle Nova structure shaped like a doublewide where she dropped off the vampire, she turns to the paltry group that has volunteered to defend the neighborhood.

THEY DRINK OUR BLOOD

Mike is singing—Pearl Jam, by the sound of the garbled words. Clay's skeletal, pallid face nearly glows beneath one of the sparse streetlights, and Lisa wonders when she last saw him in the sun.

Koko wants to keep walking past the entry, but Lisa tugs the leash and the dog leads the way up the makeshift wooden ramp, bounding over the sunken section. At the plywood double doors, Lisa turns back.

"How are we gonna—"

Mike shoves past her, turning the knob and shouldering through the door. Koko charges behind him, dragging Lisa inside, filling her lungs with dust. An electric camping lantern on an upside-down bucket lights the room in chiaroscuro. Faces are obscured in contrasting shadow. She sees it as a quick flash of a camera, a moment that quickly flicks to the next. Wood planks stacked on the floor. Frayed tarps hanging from the exposed beams.

"Who invited Grandpa?"

The shiny blade of an axe swings through the diffuse light. A crunch. Blood spatter mirrors the arc of the blade. Falling to the floor, a face sliced near in half, a smile deeper than Glasgow etched into a cratered cheek. Cracked teeth bounce off Lisa's boot.

A shrill scream. Koko's guttural barks. A rough hand grabbing at hers.

"Give me the dog."

Wolf pulls Koko toward the door, threads the leash through the two upright metal handles, ties a knot, seals the exit. No escape.

Bodies at her back push her farther into the room. The seated forms are now standing, backing away against the peeling wall. Koko growls, barks, slobber flying, droplets speckling the writhing creature on the floor, clutching his broken face.

A shadowed figure creeps against the tarp, moving toward the door.

"You, cripple; stay here. Don't let anyone out." Wolf's gruff voice commands from behind her back.

Jodi leaps over the injured vampire, tackles the shadow figure into the tarp, tearing a side of it down from the ceiling. Elevated a yard or so off the ground on some stack of debris under the cloth, Jodi's hand jerks Lisa's chisel with Norman Bates aggression.

Crack.

Scream.

Crack.

Scream.

Crack.

Sputter.

"Suck on this, you filthy vampire trash!" Jodi shoves a fistful of garlic into the vampire's mouth, turning its farm animal squeals into coughs. She thrusts her hand over the thing's mouth, and now the only sounds it makes are its feet kicking the cabinet.

No more screams left, Lisa's sophomore year sculpture class tool continues its rhythmic recoil and stab.

Autumn straddles the half-faced vampire on the floor, stake raised above her head.

She heaves the stake and her full weight down onto the wailing creature's rib cage. The stake splinters, failing to pierce even the T-shirt.

"Shit!" Autumn panics, stabbing with little force at a rapid clip, the vampire wriggling his hips, desperately trying to shake her off. The disfigured vampire on the floor blindly flails its arms, leaving its own blood on Autumn's neck.

Three shadowed vampires cower against the wall opposite the barred entry. Mike jams the butt end of the axe into a chin.

He yanks the semiconscious vampire by its long hair to a short cabinet on the front wall. The limp female sits on the cabinet, head lolling. Mike grabs her shirt collar.

"Someone help me with him!" Autumn's shrill command pierces the growling, barking, moaning, screaming sounds of bones crunching, arteries bursting, blouses ripping.

As her left knee hits the floor, Lisa's right arm punches *The Gift* into what's left of the vampire's face after Mike demolished it with the axe upon arrival. Blood, teeth, skin, pieces of the human body not covered in any Anatomy for Artists texts spurt from the cratered face into hers. The third strike bursts an eyeball. What's left of the mouth gapes like Francis Bacon's *Pope Innocent X*, screaming a pain so deep there are no words. The weight of *The Gift* fatigues Lisa's arm. One more short punch into the neck makes a fountain of blood, streaking her face like Bacon's paint drips, and the ruined head moves no more.

Two vampires leap over the now faceless vampire's now still legs. Autumn reaches to grab an ankle but hugs only air. Koko growls and gnashes her teeth, sending the two skittering to a halt before they can charge the door. Clay rips the blade from his cane.

"Fucking gross! Fucking undead, pervert! This thing's got a dick!"

Wolf lunges across the room to Mike's disgusted shouts. "Hold it down!"

One hand on each end, Mike shoves the axe handle into the vampire's neck, pinning its head back. The skirt pulled down to the knees keeps the legs kicking up and down like a fishtail.

"Don't you fucking move, you filthy bloodsucking freak," Mike spits into the vampire's face. As Wolf's curved blade carves into his exposed genitals, slicing into the base at the pelvic bone, the vampire's whole body convulses. The force of his neck against the handle smashes the now apparent Adam's apple. His involuntary hip thrusts don't interrupt Wolf from severing the soft, fleshy unit, letting it drop to the floor with a squishy plop in a deluge of blood.

What appears to be a male vampire—though who knows at this point?—steps toward Koko. The dog surges forward, locking her teeth into loose denim. The vampire tumbles to the floor, taking his female companion down with him, kicking until Koko releases her fangs.

If there was any doubt the creatures in this room were something other than human, it's erased by the bellow. Bestial, a wolf's cry strangled through a mouth meant for words is at once familiar and alien.

"Shut this thing up." Wolf backs away from the undead eunuch, just far enough from Mike's swinging axe.

The vampire couple attempt to scramble to their feet, just out of reach of Koko's snarl, as Lisa winds up like a shot putter and smashes the tapered end of the iron into the male's temple. The impact knocks him into her and sends them both back to the ground.

Cane tossed to the floor, Clay throws his thin frame onto the couple, stabbing the semi-conscious male in the chest. The female, seated with her back pressed against a metal filing cabinet, wriggles to free herself from the exsanguinating male flopping between her akimbo legs. He presses his weakening hands over his heart in a pathetic attempt to stop the bleeding.

Mike's axe opens the now sexless thing's face like a hot dog bun. With a crack and a squelch, the animal wail cuts off, leaving the higher-pitched cries of the vampires masquerading as human women's squeals.

"Give me a better weapon." Autumn tugs at Lisa's backpack strap. Lisa sheds the bag.

Lisa's backpack clatters on the floor. Autumn slices the saw, another relic from Sculpture 1, into the swiveling neck of the vampire buried under her mate. Blood spills but doesn't spray. Clay pulls the vampire's head back by her long curls.

Kneeling on the floor, Autumn saws into the female thing's throat. The shrieks have become gurgles. A soft, rhythmic, synthetic sound rises from somewhere in the room. Under Koko's barks, Lisa can't place it.

"Hey, Mike, this one's got the right parts." Jodi yanks a small vampire from the shadows of the rear wall by the arm with such violence her neck nearly collides with the blade Wolf points at it. Her clothes are shredded, hanging as fringe off her tiny white body. Yes, she has the right parts.

Mike approaches the pretty vampire, massaging his crotch.

"Fuck!" he shouts.

"Well, how many shots did you have?" Jodi asks.

"It's not that. It's that fucking dirty thing over there. That's all I can think of. Fucking filthy vampire."

"It's all right. I've got something long and hard for her." Bloody chisel in hand, Jodi winds up like she's about to pitch a softball. Mike and Wolf hold the lithe, exposed vampire down by her shoulders.

The type of scream only Edvard Munch could imagine fills the stale air as Jodi pulls the chisel from between the vampire's skinny legs. She shortens her windup and plunges it right back in. Again and again until the screams fade to groans and then it's just flesh tearing and organs popping and that soft, repeating scraping sound.

Lisa approaches the tarp. A phone is ringing. She grabs the tarp with one hand, holds it taut, and digs the sharp nails of *The Gift* into it, tearing it down like a claw.

Two vampires huddle on the floor. The girl thing has a phone to her ear.

A muffled voice is asking, "What's your emergency?"

Wolf reaches through the hole in the tarp, pulls the phone from her hand.

"Of course they're calling the cops," Lisa says. "They control them."

THEY DRINK OUR BLOOD

"That's why we're here." Wolf presses "end," shines the phone's flashlight on the two.

"Shit. Give me a new weapon; I'm not reaching in there to get that chisel back." Jodi approaches the hole in the tarp.

Mike releases the naked vampire. She collapses sideways from her seat on the filing cabinet, tumbling to a floor that's as dirty as she is.

Jodi pushes Lisa's scissors into the vampire's chin just enough to make her crane her long dancer's neck. "How about this one, Mike? She's prettier than that one. I bet she's seduced so many human men over her centuries sucking blood. How many did she suck dry with a pretty face like this?"

"Please, I'm just a kid," she stammers, her voice soft and tiny. Some TikTokers were wondering if vampires can feel emotions as we do. It's obvious they can experience fear. And they lie in the face of it for self-preservation, as we do.

Jodi pushes the scissor point further into her chin, forcing the vampire to her feet.

"What do you think?"

Mike stares at the creature, slender and tall, with her eternal youth gained by draining it from others. The cockroach that lives forever. He swings the axe into her ribs. A crack and a squish and a shout of "No!" from behind the torn curtain and Jodi hops back as the vampire tips over, blood gushing from the ragged indentation in her side.

The final vampire in his blue hoodie throws his arms into a V overhead. And this time, without the mirrors to hide behind, Lisa sees his face. Not the face from his Uber rider profile. His real face. In the spotlight of Goya's black period, his shiny white fangs curl over his lips, and she sees blood dripping from some recent kill. His eyes bulging wide, mouth curling into the snarl of a wolf, about to speak or bite.

Lisa doesn't give him a chance. Arm outstretched, she swings *The Gift* into his monstrous face, swiping the nails across his tapered cheek, tearing through the flesh to the teeth. It takes a split second for the blood to flow, and when it does, it's a waterfall. His hands fly to his face with the speed that's made his kind so hard to kill, but the blood spills through his long fingers.

Lisa turns to the door, assuming for a moment the whimper and spittle-choked sputter is coming from Koko. With the sudden stillness in the room, the dog is silent, only the rattle of her collar as she shakes her head to try to free herself of the persistent vampire blood spattered on her fur. She sinks down to the floor, relaxed finally or out of energy, to play dead with the others.

The animal noise comes from the vampire who calls himself Kaden, his frayed cheek gushing blood. Standing behind the kneeling vampire, Wolf grabs his braids, pulling his head back, exposing his neck like the creature must have done to so many innocents before taking a bite. Wolf's blade slices cleanly across the neck. At the Adam's apple, he digs deeper, inserting the pointed end into the throat. Slimy chunks drop down on the hoodie in a cascade of blood. Wolf saws at the throat.

The vampire is limp, hands dangling at his sides, jaw slack, mouth agape. Wolf's hand saws back and forth, mechanical like a third-seat cellist performing a piece for the show after the matinee. Until he hits bone. A couple of aggressive, muscular strokes of the blade fail to sever the vertebrae.

Wolf lifts the vampire by his hair, presenting his near decapitated, disfigured, bloody head in lighting reminiscent of Caravaggio's *David and Goliath*. They have slayed giants here tonight.

Wolf releases his hand, and the body thuds to the floor. Koko scrambles back to her feet from her short nap.

"The bloodsuckers all dead?" Mike cradles the blunt end of the axe, ready to strike the moment one of these fiends pops back to un-life with a banshee wail like in the movies.

But the room is silent, just the neglected floor creaking under their feet.

Autumn is first to speak. "We should probably do that to all of them, right? Cut their heads off?"

"At least stab them through their hearts. Some cultures kill them that way. Some cut their heads off. Some light them on fire, but I don't think we wanna do that or we'd destroy our neighborhood and not be much better than them—"

"We are better than them regardless, Lisa." Jodi rummages through the backpack. "We don't drink blood. We don't kill people. There's nothing fucking sharp in here."

An X-Acto knife in her hand, she abandons the bag. Lisa takes her place, shining her iPhone flashlight into the bag. There are sharp things in here. She doesn't need more blood on her hands.

THEY DRINK OUR BLOOD

Mike swings the axe into the near naked vampire's neck. With a soft slosh and a robust thud, the head tips from where it leaned against the wall, the chin landing on the clavicle. Stand a bottle wrapped in brown paper between her legs (hide the little bit of bloody chisel handle poking out) and she'd present as any number of sots in the doorway of the many empty storefronts on Carson.

The head isn't fully severed, but they move on to the castrated thing. Lisa searches the bag for the other wooden stake. Maybe it will be more resilient when the vampire isn't fighting back.

Clay stabs his sharp object into the heart of the female playing the role of Mary in the *Pietà* by the door. Autumn digs the saw into the neck of the imitation Jesus, failing to achieve the grotesque depths of Wolf's hunting knife. Blood spills from the growing wound, barely deeper than the flesh.

She gets down on one knee, recruiting more power from her hips as she saws back and forth. As Lisa learned in sculpture class, maintaining a straight line when sawing is harder than it looks, even with the wood clamped to the table.

The vampire's head hangs to the side, and Autumn's cuts are an abstract expressionist disaster. Ragged skin falls off the body like papier-mâché.

Clay covers his mouth, but as he convulses and reaches for the wall for support, the beer-scented vomit has unobstructed flow onto the *Pieta,* tiny chunks mingling with the blood in Autumn's blonde hair and her pink top.

"Ugh! This is so much worse than the blood!"

"Sorry." Clay wipes his mouth.

Koko lurches from the door, toward the *pietà,* barking with enthusiasm she hasn't shown since the eight vampires were ambulatory or since she last detected someone approaching Lisa's studio door.

"Stop it, Koko," Lisa says, but she sees the glow around the old blinds on the two front windows. She hugs the blood-spattered dog until Koko quiets then creeps toward the window, peeks through the inch-wide gap between the dusty plastic blind and the grime-coated frame.

"Cops?" Jodi asks.

"No. Ride share."

And it's only because the collectively held breath has barely the time to be expelled that they can hear the soft pulse of a phone vibration. The phone glows through the front pocket of the faceless vampire sprawled on the floor.

"Your ride's here, bloodsucker motherfucker." Mike laughs, the wet guffaw filling the forsaken space, silent aside from the low, constant buzz of the lantern now toppled to the floor with its flimsy paint bucket table and the purr of the engine idling outside.

Jodi elbows him in the ribs and raises her saw. "Be ready in case the driver comes in."

"Drivers don't do that." Lisa keeps her gaze fixed on the red sedan. If the obscured driver can see her, she must look like a disembodied head on the side of the wall. "They wait five minutes, then they leave. They can't afford to waste time going in and out of houses. Plus, it could be dangerous."

Mike sputter-laughs again. "What kind of vampire calls a cab anyway? Can't they turn into bats and fly away?"

"Maybe this one doesn't know how yet. They gotta learn like everything else, right?" Autumn has fetched the broken stake from the shadows, uses it in a futile attempt to comb Clay's stomach contents from her hair.

"How do we know the driver's not another familiar?" Jodi takes a step toward the door, closer to Lisa.

"Or it's just a driver doing a job." Lisa glances back at the sedan, still idling, the driver still hidden in the shadows.

"Bloodsucking freaks control everything else. Why shouldn't they get their spindly, filthy hands on ride share?" She takes another step.

"Sure, maybe at the top, but we drivers don't know anything. We're just gig workers. We don't even have health insurance or a W2 or anything like that, so we're not—"

"Oh that's right!" Clay smacks himself in the forehead in mocking self-effacement, inadvisable, as any impact could release more vodka-suspended chunks. "Didn't you drive one of these vampires down here yourself?"

Autumn stops combing her hair. Wolf and Mike look up from the vampire, the one with all the new orifices in his chest and abdomen courtesy of Jodi and the chisel before it was lost in his co-conspirator, and stop searching his blood-drenched pockets.

"Yeah, but I told you where to find them so we could stop them. I led you here. I wouldn't do that if I was involved with them, would I?"

THEY DRINK OUR BLOOD

"You ask us to get into a vampire brain?" Mike spits. "Where's the axe?"

Wolf reaches under the drop cloth covering what seems to have once been a desk and hands Mike the axe by its viscera-spattered wooden handle.

The driver waits only five minutes. How long has it been? Lisa talks. Nonsense, filibustering about ride-share practices, secrets of drivers, anything that enters her mind while she counts the seconds. It can't be much longer now, only two minutes surely until the car pulls away and they abandon their delusions, chalking it up to some hero's high paranoia even if they don't acknowledge it in words.

The high. Surveying the room with her strong ocular emotional connection, she feels it too. Like gazing at Rothko's canvas, it assures her that someone else, even someone who fled pogroms in Russia, shared the same emotions as a teenager who'd never left the time zone, the work of the room is for all of humanity. This *Guernica* is her gift, her contribution the squares could never make in their muddled message. But it's not about a shared feeling; it's a shared existence.

It needs to be done again. As many times as possible. A magnum opus. Because Picasso didn't stop at *Guernica*. He may never have topped it, but he continued to create. As she would as well. She had to. She just hadn't found her voice, her unique style until now. There was no movement. No Apollonaire to put a name to it. No confederation of like-minded people. That was the problem. She had been looking for artists. Keeping herself confined to art. But art is not found just in galleries. Her collaborators who would shape the course of human history were found in a bar. At random. Maybe like the café in Paris that spawned surrealism.

If they don't turn on her now. Approaching with axes, stakes, and knives. Closing in. Can't be much longer. How quickly the five minutes had moved when she was the one in the driver's seat, scrolling Facebook. Now, the longer she waits, the more these seconds stretch to minutes, the tighter her chest, the shallower her breath. Breath as shallow as the decorative arts movement.

And words, any words that will keep the knives and axes and stakes dangling at their sides tumble from her mouth. What has she said to them? She doesn't know. Nothing that would make them think she's a vampire. It's all too true. All too human. Connection.

LUCY LEITNER

The soft thrum of the phone in the lifeless vampire's pocket halts the Van Helsing march. Almost coordinated, the engine revs. The light glowing around the blinds, through the thick, dusty pane turns from white to red before fading away.

They resume their tasks; riffling through pockets, chopping off heads. Lisa inhales until her heart slows, then she joins them.

Autumn lies naked on the bar, elbow and hip no doubt bathing in warm beer and all manner of grime, but still cleaner than the vampire blood and slimy nuggets of internal components that kept them undead until tonight. Not that Autumn's clothes were any more squalid than the others (except for Wolf, whose black jeans, black shirt, and leather jacket were miraculously immaculate); she just lacked their modesty. Even Mike had only stripped down to his red boxer briefs, his Miller High Life bubbling down his sarcopenic chest and bulbous, hops-filled stomach from their arrival back at Jake's Mistake when he'd treated the bottle as if it really was the champagne of beers.

Their clothes were soaking in the derelict kitchen sink so as not to arouse suspicion when they finally journeyed home. Lisa, Jodi, and Clay remained clothed, deciding to risk being seen when they finally returned to their apartments in the wee hours when their neighbors would still be cowering. And even if they were spotted? Well, their selfless deed would be major news by then. They wouldn't have to explain when the media reported the triumph of humanity in that abandoned office.

Lisa sips her beer, eyes glued to the TV.

"Maybe we should have lit the whole thing on fire." Next to Lisa at the bar, Jodi shakes her head. "Least they'd've found it by now. Something'd be on the news."

"But would they get it with the stakes turned to ashes? Bodies all charred, would they be able to tell they were vampires?"

From her *Olympia* pose, Autumn throws her head back and laughs. "They'll find it eventually. Don't sweat it. Celebrate! It's a party!"

Lisa smiles, raises her Straub, appeases Autumn enough that she pours the Fireball she'd been sipping from the bottle into her belly button.

"No way that's the only lair," Jodi says.

"Couple nights back I seen a big group of what looked like teenagers down in the parking lot under the bridge. Y'know where they put in that bike path a few years back?" Wolf says.

"That's just a couple blocks from where we found the others tonight."

"What'd the kids look like?" Lisa asks.

"Like kids. Swarthy-looking creeps."

"How were they dressed?"

"Like teenagers. But from when you were a teenager."

"Like they're stuck in the best time of their lives. Last time they were actually alive," Lisa says.

A silly song plays about parking a car in the front yard that Lisa is amazed every time to hear 30 years after its radio heyday. Mike slurps the cinnamon schnapps from the stripper's belly button.

"That's an open space under the bridge. Better wait till they head back to their dens just before sunup. Can't have 'em turning into bats and flying away," Jodi says.

"They didn't turn into bats tonight. Maybe that's just a superstition," Lisa says.

"Or maybe those were newer vampires that didn't have the skill yet. Why they called a ride. We can't be too sure."

"No, we can't." Lisa reaches for *The Gift*, its iron body dyed with red splotches. The nonsensical object that finally served its "ironic" purpose sits on the bar, waiting to be called into action again to defend her against her enemies. "And you're right. That space is way too open. They could turn into mist, too. Or wolves. We've gotta get them where they can't get out. In their coffins would be ideal, you know—"

"Think you can trail them to where they rest?" Jodi turns to Wolf.

"Sure, and if I lose them, we can always lure them out with your smooth, white neck." Beneath his thick, graying beard the hint of a smile.

"Clay, you wanna body shot?"

"No way!" Autumn play-smacks Mike's arm. "He already puked on me once!"

Lisa gazes back up at the TV as the commercial cuts back into the 11 o'clock WTF News. Tinny music plays from Mike's phone to keep the noise down to stave off any potential customers, and Autumn's drunken giggles fade. The bar blurs and warps around the transparent tube connecting Lisa to the TV mounted high on the wall, the words at the bottom of the screen the only thing in her vision.

"Vampire hoax."

The anchor speaks. "Netflix star Ty Denning has been charged today with filing a false police report. Last week, the actor, in town filming *Working Stiffs,* claimed he was attacked by two vampires in the parking lot of a South Side bar. According to police, an extra on the set came forward claiming that Denning attempted to pay him to act as a vampire in a staged attack behind the bar from which he'd been ejected the night before. The extra refused, but two others, whose names are currently being withheld, accepted. Police say that upon questioning, the two confessed to staging the attack."

The broadcast cuts to a weather map. Jodi's voice pops the bubble, bringing Lisa back to the bar.

"Fuck that Hollywood asshole. Now the cops will have more reason to think vampires don't exist."

Lisa stares straight ahead, while inside she screams with the primal emotion only expressed in distorted faces, aggressive brushstrokes, and unnatural colors. The threat will never vanish, just continue to insinuate itself into our institutions, eating us away from within.

She dips a napkin into her Straub to wipe the blood from one of the pins in T*he Gift.*

"It's a good thing they've got us."

ART REFERENCED

1. Salvador Dalí: The Persistence of Memory
2. Walter Sickert: The Camden Town Murder
3. John Singer Sargent: Carnation, Lily, Lily, Rose
4. Pablo Picasso: Desmoiselles D'Avignon
5. Edward Hopper: Nighthawks
6. Eugène Delacroix: Liberty Leading the People
7. Salvador Dalí: Lobster Telephone
8. Edvard Munch: The Scream
9. Édouard Manet: Luncheon on the Grass
10. Hieronymus Bosch: The Garden of Earthly Delights
11. Sandro Botticelli: The Birth of Venus
12. René Magritte: The Son of Man
13. Claude Monet: Water Lillies
14. Berthe Morisot: Julie Manet and her Greyhound Laerte
15. Johannes Vermeer: Girl with a Pearl Earring
16. Francisco Goya: Saturn Devouring His Son
17. Leonardo da Vinci: Mona Lisa
18. Gustav Klimt: Adam and Eve
19. Salvador Dalí: The Burning Giraffe
20. René Magritte: The False Mirror
21. Vincent van Gogh: Self-Portrait with Bandaged Ear
22. William Blake: The Ghost of a Flea
23. Frida Kahlo: Girl with Death Mask
24. Salvador Dalí: The Elephants
25. John Singer Sargent: *Madame X*
26. Jacques-Louis David: The Death of Marat
27. René Magritte: Young Girl Eating a Bird
28. René Magritte: Empire of Light
29. Andy Warhol: Campbell's Soup Cans
30. Vincent van Gogh: The Starry Night
31. Vincent van Gogh: The Potato Eaters
32. Marcel Duchamp: Nude Descending a Staircase (No. 2)
33. René Magritte: The Balcony
34. Mark Rothko: 403
35. Henri de Toulouse-Lautrec: Jane Avril
36. Francis Bacon: Study after Velázquez's Portrait of Pope Innocent X
37. Francisco Goya: The Third of May 1808
38. Michelangelo Buonarroti: The Pietà
39. Pablo Picasso: Guernica
40. Édouard Manet: Olympia
41. Man Ray: The Gift

Join Blood Bound Books
Newsletter to receive 20% off your
next order at
www.BloodBoundBooks.com

ABOUT THE AUTHOR

Lucy Leitner is the author of five previous novels and a short story collection. Her fiction has appeared in six anthologies. She lives in Pittsburgh, PA.

lucyleitner.com